Paper Cranes

JULIE JAMES

Paper Cranes. Copyright © 2021 by Julie L. James. All rights reserved. Printed in the United States of America. No part of this book may be used or reproduced in any manner whatsoever without written permission except in the case of brief quotations embodied in critical articles and reviews.

Book Design and Illustrations by Jessica Slater

ISBN (paperback): 9798457561885

For Tyler

Prologue

" Just set it all over there."

"Are you sure?" asked the nurse.

"Yes." I replied.

I barely glanced at the pile of my husband's belongings that were stacked up on the chair next to the hospital bed where he lay. My eyes were cloudy under my heavy eyelids and surprisingly dry. Andrew was dead. His car was obliterated by an 18-wheeler 12 hours earlier while he was driving home from work. His body was crushed and he died almost instantly but they brought him to the hospital by helicopter in case there was a chance.

Once I heard the news of the accident from Andrew's father, I knew there wasn't a chance. I had a sinking feeling in the pit of my stomach that the phone call was delivering irreversible bad news.

I sucked in a large breath, forbade my father-in-law from telling the children the news, and rushed to the hospital. My entire body began to shake as I approached the outside of the hospital room; the harsh lights shone down on me illuminating my every movement. Andrew was almost unrecognizable: his face was swollen, coated in blood, his entire right side looked collapsed, twisted, and bent in all the wrong directions. I couldn't even tell what shirt he had put on that day because it was so drenched in blood and filthy. He wasn't breathing even though there were tubes coming out of his nose and mouth. What was visible of his skin was devoid of color and flat. I didn't recognize him except for his hands. His hands were perfectly clean, the same shape, size, and color they always are. His silver ring was perfectly intact and completely spotless.

I walked over to Andrew's left side and gently tugged the ring off of his finger. It slid off too quickly and bounced off of the floor tiles. It caught the light as I picked it up so I could see that the inscription was still perfectly there and had hardly worn off the way mine had. Andrew almost never wore his ring and it still looked brand new. He only wore it for formal occasions and some more important work events. Today was supposed to be one of his larger presentations so he must have decided to slip his ring on while I was still asleep between our alarms going off.

I slipped his ring into my pocket while monitors beeped and blinked in the small hospital room. I met with doctors, nurses, and undertakers throughout the entire rest of the day as his body lay still and lifeless next to me. Andrew's parents came after settling the children, lying to them about work going long for both of us. I realized I hadn't left the hospital room for hours until they arrived. They looked like strangers, people I had never met and had never spoken with before. The amount of grief they carried on their faces and in the way they walked in somehow felt more soul-crushingly sad to me then my inexplicable pain and emptiness. The hollow feeling was evident in the way Andrew's mother looked at him as she bent down to hug him and in the way his father couldn't face taking a close look at the hospital bed. Howls of anguish overtook the air all around me; I could hear nothing else. As I watched them crumble onto the tiles of the hospital floor, I felt the pain of seeing Andrews body covered in blood, and realized he was gone all over again. I felt my heart shatter like glass within my chest.

Once all of Andrew's things were gathered up in my arms, his mother reached out to take them from me. I gave her everything so that I could sign papers. The three of us began to walk out of the room together toward home. I froze. I couldn't leave Andrew there alone all night. He would be so cold, so alone. The hospital room had felt like my new home. I couldn't just walk away.

I had to physically force myself to step away from the room, shuffling slowly down the hallway in a daze. I approached the double doors that secured the wing of the third floor where my husband lay. I heaved into a tall, gray trash can more times than I could count, gasping for air, shuttering, and shivering. My body felt like it was just a vertical stack of bones and nothing else. It was like I had no organs, no skin, no body. Only bones.

I arrived home at our house. My friend Ruth was standing on the flagstone path that led up to the front door. She looked pale, but prepared for my arrival home. She said nothing while she held me in an embrace for what felt like hours before dragging me upstairs and tucking my shaking body into bed.

After 12 straight hours of sleep, I woke up to a dark cloud of missed phone calls and a bright day of sunshine that blasted through my window and almost blinded my sensitive eyes. I reached in my jean pocket and felt that Andrew's ring was still there, good as new, and completely spotless.

Chapter 1

CASSIE

"I think we should break up. I've thought about it and you aren't ever going to be the person I get married to so why should I bother wasting any of our time and emotions anymore? Do you know what I'm saying? Like, really what are we even doing with each other? Like, why are we together? Why do we really think that this will go anywhere other than completely south?"

I was standing on the curb outside of the parking lot below my dorm apartment on my cell phone breaking up with my boyfriend Jack who was 20 hours away in Colorado at his college studying and going rock climbing for fun. I had become so unbelievably bored with the scheduled phone calls, the mundane updates on how our classes are going, and the complete lack of chemistry.

"Where is this coming from?" Jack stuttered.

"I just don't think I see a future for us and I don't want to delay a breakup any longer. I know it will only hurt more if we wait on this." I replied confidently.

I had already waited a month longer than I meant to for this break-up conversation.

"Are you seriously doing this over the phone, Cassie?" he pleaded.

"What was I supposed to do, Jack? Fly hours to see you? Spend hundreds on a plane ticket so that we can be together in person for this? That's the most absurd logic I've ever heard of." I said.

"Yes! That's how decent people end serious relationships, Cassie!" he said.

"I really don't see the value in doing this in person and I'm really sorry if you feel like I am springing this on you. You aren't The One, Jack. You just aren't and I'm sorry." I said.

I sensed Jack's frustration from hours away before he even spoke again.

"I just refuse to give up on us this abruptly, Cassie. I really don't want this to end and I'll do anything to keep what we have going. What can I do to change your mind?" he begged.

His tone shifted from being annoyed and hurt, to sad and desperate. I really needed this conversation to end so I continued the honesty streak I started.

"There's nothing you can do, Jack. There is so much more to me than this relationship and I really wouldn't mind exploring other elements of my life that don't include you. I've already missed out of so much at college this year because I feel like you're holding me back. Please don't ask me if there's anything you can do because there really isn't."

Next, I went in for the absolute worst thing you can ever suggest during a break-up and I began already hating myself for saying it out loud.

"Can we still be friends?" I said, cringing as I spoke.

I could feel all signs of hope leaving Jack's body and soul from states away the second the words came out of my mouth.

"No. No, Cassie. I can't be friends with you and I don't want to break up. Please don't do this." he said.

"It's done and I'm sorry and I hope you understand what a great guy I think you are. You didn't do anything wrong and I need you to know that. Please stay in touch and reach out if you ever think we can be friends in the future. I love you Jack. Goodbye."

I hung up without giving him a chance to say another word and slowly pressed the air I'd forgotten to exhale between my lips. I had been pacing the curb and was starting to get beyond cold in the dim February night. It was nearly ten at night and I still had to finish writing a paper.

I felt a little sad, a little relieved, but mostly tired. I really didn't want to hurt Jack, or myself for that matter, but the relationship had run its course. We had met over the past summer at a party and immediately hit it off. He was so interesting to me. I'd always had a thing for really tall guys; at six feet and two inches, he stood almost a foot taller than me, and really knew how to tell a funny story. The first thing I overheard him talking about was his solo sail across a massive lake in Michigan and how he meticulously avoided smashing into rocks during a blinding squall and had single-handedly assisted another sailor who was lost in another area of the lake, using only sailing charts, and no GPS at all. Old school ways of navigation had always been impressive to me and I was instantly attracted. Jack got my number that night and took me to dinner almost a week later.

Summer with Jack was an absolute blast and it didn't hurt that my job as a lifeguard had me the most fit and tan I'd ever been in my entire life and feeling great about it. Dating Jack was good until it was boring. He had to fly all the way back to Colorado for school while I returned to Pennsylvania to my college. The first semester went well with fun phone call updates and hilarious stories about ridiculous friends. Jack actually had one of the most incredible groups of guy friends I had ever had the pleasure of hearing on the other end of the phone. From what I heard about them, they sounded truly awesome. I was enamoured with their stories and cross-country adventures and genuinely great personalities even though I never got to meet them in person. But, things had become boring to me after we spent Christmas break together. Once interesting stories became redundant, and keeping up with the time change was annoying. I had a demanding class schedule this semester and really lost all inspiration with Jack. He wasn't serious enough about a career after college and it was clear to me that he wasn't going to grow in the way I needed him to anytime soon. I imagined him living in a sailboat forever instead of just having one to sail for fun. He would want to rock climb or try craft beers every weekend instead of pursuing another degree or building a house or having a family. It was a summer fling that went on too long and had no lasting power from the way I saw it.

I wanted more than fun. I had really high standards for my future and didn't keep them a secret. I wanted a career, a house, a family, and inspiration. Just one of those things wasn't enough and Jack was never going to measure up to the type of man I needed in order to accomplish all of my life goals.

I decided to take a short walk around my apartment building and passed at least three other couples who held hands in the cold air. I knew I had made the right decision ending things but it still hurt. *Do I have expectations that are out-of-this-world-way-too-high?* I thought.

There's no way. I'm not crazy for wanting a real life filled with inspiration and meaning.

I decided not to question myself again and headed toward the entrance of the building. As I stepped up to the sidewalk I made sure to look down to ensure that there was salt, and not ice, beneath my feet. As I was watching my step, I slammed squarely into an ice cold and hard as a rock telephone pole and fell completely backwards into the parking lot, smacking my head off of the salty, slushy pavement.

I screamed in anguish. It was so cold and so dark. My forehead throbbed in excruciating pain. Two out of the three other couples who were somehow still outside in the freezing night came running toward me. I looked straight ahead, directly into the winter sky and watched snowflakes slowly float in the air. The two couples' faces appeared right over me with concerned expressions.

"Are you OK?" a girl asked.

"Dude, we watched you slam right into that pole, are you drunk?" her boyfriend asked.

"Do you need us to call 911?"

"Your face is already bruising and you will totally have a goose egg."

"Oh yeah, there's definitely gonna be a goose egg..."

I slowly got to my feet without anyone's help, not that they were offering.

"I'm fine." I said as I walked inside in a daze.

I definitely had a concussion and I still had to write my paper for class.

I could hardly see straight as I started walking up the four flights of stairs to my apartment. I stumbled at least three times up the steps and hung onto the railing for dear life, actively fighting waves of nausea. A group of guys came running down the stairs in my direction. One of them slowed down and placed his hand on my elbow to help me.

"Hard night? You OK?" he asked.

"Yes." I said without looking up.

"Are you drunk?" he asked.

"No way! It's Tuesday, Sir." I said.

"That doesn't stop most people and I wouldn't judge you if you were." he laughed.

"Seriously, I'm not drunk, I swear. I just ran into a telephone pole and now I can't see anything normally. Like everything is actually gray and shades of brown instead of colors." I explained.

"Well, you are in the dorm stairwell. Gray and brown are the only colors in here. Plus, it's really dark outside so there's no natural light coming in to soften the place up." he said.

I could hear him smiling as he continued to help guide me up the stairs. He was mostly a blur to me, but I noticed him signaling to his friends to head on without him, indicating that he would catch up with them. I tried to focus my eyes on his face but my vision wouldn't let me see anything above chest level. From what I could see, he was fairly tall, seemed strong, and had great taste in jackets.

Most college guys would wear hoodies with or without varsity jackets in winter even if it was snowing or below freezing. But this guy was wearing an actual Helly Hanson winter coat made for snow activities. I had to see his face. I tried once more to glance up at him and started to stumble again. He grabbed my hand this time.

"What apartment are you in?" he asked.

"4G." I replied.

"I'm helping you get home unless you think you should go to the hospital instead. You have a major goose egg on your forehead." he said.

"If one more person says the word 'goose egg' to me tonight I'm going to die. Who are you?" I asked.

"I'm Andrew. I don't live on this side of campus so I actually don't know where 4G is, but I will take you there. What do you have against the word 'goose egg'? It's just a phrase everyone says."

"It's stupid and everyone who uses it is stupid. I can't help you find 4G Andrew, because I can't see anything right now. You look like nothing. I can only see your coat and I want you to know that I respect you for wearing it." I said.

"Thanks? Why do you respect me for wearing a coat? I think this way is E through L..."

I was thankful that he was reading the signs in the hallway. I definitely wouldn't be able to read them, and couldn't quite figure out where I was in the building.

"Because real men wear coats in winter and little boys wear hoodies when it's 20 degrees outside." I said.

We had reached the outside of my apartment that I shared with two other girls. Awesome, awesome friends I met three years before at Freshman orientation and would live with forever if I could. I recognized the welcome mat with the Weiner dogs in hot dog costumes exchanging Valentines. It was so tacky that Ruth, Jennifer, and I had to have it.

"What's your code?" he asked, reaching for the door.

"Um...I...I can't remember...I don't know...um...let me think..." I stuttered.

"Is it four digits or five?" he asked.

"I have no idea. I seriously can't remember it right now. My head isn't working...is it four or five digits?" I asked.

"That's what I'm asking you." he said.

"What are you asking me?" I asked.

"What's your name? Do you know what day it is?" he asked.

"Cassie. Cassie Bond." I replied.

"OK, sure. I bet it is 'Cassie Bond'. You definitely have a concussion." he said.

"No, seriously! My last name really is Bond! Also, I think it's Thursday." I said.

"Earlier you said it was Tuesday. Which it is. It actually is Tuesday, Cassie...if that's even your real first name. There's no way your last name is actually 'Bond'. Do you seriously think it's Thursday right now? What number am I holding up?" he asked.

I tried to look up at him again and it was still so blurry. I could make out more of his features but still couldn't focus on his face. I could see that he had dark hair and a symmetrical face but that was about it. I tried to look at his hand but it was completely blurred. I reached out to his wrist to hold his hand closer to me. Four. He was definitely holding up four fingers.

"Four." I declared.

"You're wrong. It's three. Can you seriously not see that I'm holding up three?" he asked.

"What did you say your name was?" I asked.

I couldn't remember anything all of a sudden.

How many digits was my code? Who is this guy? What's his name? Why does my head hurt so much?

"It's Andrew. We just met. Cassie, are you OK?"

His blurry face looked concerned from what I could see of it. He looked to the left and then to the right, probably for one of my roommates or hallmates to help him get this crazy and confused girl with a goose egg on her forehead out of his life so he could get back to his friends. He began knocking on the door of my apartment rapidly.

I looked down at my own hands. I could see them so clearly. *Maybe if he put his hands down next to mine, I would be able to see how many fingers he's holding up.* I grabbed his wrist again, and focused deeply on his hands.

"Five. You're definitely holding up five fingers now, Andrews." I said confidently.

"It's Andrew. Not Andrews. You really need some help. Do you have a phone on you and can call someone to let you in or give you the code? Do you want me to take you to the hospital?" he asked.

"I do have a phone. Yes. Yes. A phone. Here. In my coat's pockets, Andrew. Andrew, here's the phone. Are you ready for the phone, Andrew? I'm calling Ruth, Andrew. Ruth probably won't pick up though, Andrew. Andrew, she really loves dogs." I said, searching for Ruth's number.

"Great. Call Ruth and see if she can help you. My gosh, you

should see your forehead. It's really bad. The bruise is so much darker now." he said.

"RUTH! It's me Ruth. It's Cassie. Cassie Bond. I am calling you on my phone. Calling you on your phone. To tell you that I hurt my face and that Andrew needs your help. Can you call me back Ruth and help Andrew, Ruth?"

I left Ruth what I thought was an informative voicemail because I was right and Ruth didn't pick up her phone. I hoped she would call me back with this "code" Andrew kept referring to. *What's a code?*

I was so tired all of sudden and needed to no longer be standing against the wall and sat down. I'd wait for Ruth to call me back right here. I heard Andrew slide down next to me. I looked to the left and saw his face for the first time. Now that we were low to the ground I could actually make out his features. He was so handsome. He looked so much older than all the other guys at college. He had medium length dark brown hair, light brown eyes, and a very distinguished nose. Such nice teeth behind nice lips. My head came up to his shoulders as we sat next to each other so he must have been almost a foot taller than me. *So tall...*

"What are the chances of Ruth calling you back? Is there anyone else you can call? Who are your other roommates?" Andrew asked.

"So many questions, Andrew. I can't remember Jennifer's number right now."

"Is Jennifer your other roommate?" he asked.

"Yes, Andrew. No one only has one roommate." I said.

"Yeah, you're right. That would be crazy...how does your head feel?"

"It hurts a lot and I really can't remember what day it is now. Did you say it was Thursday? What time is it?" I asked.

"It's Tuesday, OO7. Let me see your phone so I can call Jennifer."

He reached out his hand for me to give him my phone. I looked at it for a moment. *Five fingers. I've still got it.* I set my hand in his. He held my hand in his for a moment before pulling my thumb away from the rest of my fingers. Warmth spread through my entire arm at the feeling of his warm palm on the back of mine. His other hand moved my thumb over toward his lap. I gasped quietly. Before I knew it, he placed my thumb on top of my phone to unlock the screen. I exhaled relief. *He needed to open my phone...*

My hand and arm felt numb, yet warm from his touch. I watched as he scrolled through the names of the contacts in my phone and found "Jennifer". He looked at me blankly as it rang. I stared up at him. I couldn't stop staring at his face as he held my phone in his hand as though it were always his. Someone answered after a few rings.

"Hey Cassie!"

"This isn't Cassie: it's Andrew and I have her phone."

"Who are you?"

"Are you home right now? Cassie fell and hit her head so I'm trying to help her get back into her apartment. Are you home or do you have a code to let us in?" he asked.

"Umm...I'm not sure who you are Andrew, but I'm definitely not giving you the code to my apartment until I know what's going on. Is Cassie OK? Can you give the phone to her?"

Andrew handed me the phone.

"Jennifer?" I asked.

"Cassie, what's going on?" she asked, sounding concerned.

"I'm OK. I just can't remember the code to get into the apartment and my head really hurts. I broke up with Jack and then I fell. I don't know anything else right now." I said.

"I'm coming over there, I'm at the library so I'll be at least ten minutes. Just stay where you are, Cassie." Jennifer explained.

She hung up and I handed the phone to Andrew. He said nothing and handed the phone right back to me.

"Andrew. I don't know you, but you can go now and thanks so much." I stated.

"I'm not going to leave you alone in a dark apartment building hallway with a head injury." he said.

"OK, but my last name really is Bond. I swear it is." I said.

Andrew said nothing and just stared at me for a few minutes. He had a concerned look on his face when he focused on my forehead with his light brown eyes. I really wished he would hold my hand again.

"Andrew." I said.

"Cassie." he said.

"Do you have anywhere to be?"

"Not really. I should study."

"What's your major?" I asked.

I can't believe it took me this long to ask him.

"Business Marketing." he said.

"How nice." I replied.

That's the most boring thing I've ever heard in my entire life, why would anyone want to take such boring classes with such boring professors? Boooorrrrriiinnnggggg.

"It's actually not boring at all." Andrew said.

"Did I just say that out loud?" I asked.

"Yes."

I started crying and I couldn't quite figure out why.

"I'm so sorry that I called your major boring and your professors boring and you're being so nice to me and your coat is so nice and my last name really is Bond. I swear. I'm so sorry. Your classes aren't actually boring."

I was crying so much and my head started to throb with a vengeance. *Where is Jennifer?* I wondered if I was in a dream but the pain in my head was so real that I knew that it couldn't have been.

"It's OK, Cassie. You don't have to apologize. You're having a hard night and I wasn't offended or anything. Why are you crying?" he asked gently.

Andrew chuckled a little as he patted my arm.

"I'm in a lot of pain and I don't know what day it is. I just dumped my boyfriend and I'm stuck in this hallway and I'm keeping you from your friends." I said.

"It's not a big deal. You don't have to apologize." he said.

"Andrew, can you keep a secret?" I asked.

"Umm..."

"I really never loved Jack and that's why I dumped him. He doesn't wear real coats like you do, Andrew. He wasn't a man. He doesn't wear real coats and I never loved him. Please don't tell him, Andrew. He would be so crushed." I said.

"I don't think you have to worry about me ever meeting this guy Jack, Cassie. You really need to get your head checked though." he said.

"I appreciate your discretion, Andrew. I'll be sure to call the doctor first thing in the morning." I said with a nod.

I took Andrew's hand in mine and held it up to my mouth. I pressed the back of his hand under his knuckles to my lips and held it there. His hand was so warm and I could feel his wrist on my cheek. Solid bones under warm skin. I didn't look up at his face but I detected slight surprise and slight amusement. I sat silently next to Andrew with his hand against my lips for an undetermined amount of time when I saw Jennifer hurriedly walking toward us from the far end of the hallway.

Andrew noticed her as well, slowly pulled his hand away from my face and stood up. I looked up to see his blurry face once again and noticed his outstretched hands. I took them and quickly rose. He was so quietly warm toward me; I tried to look into his eyes but couldn't see anything but gray and brown shapes as his face. *Why can't I see straight? My face is pounding.*

I stood in a trance, squinting at Andrew's face while Jennifer talked to him, and probably to me, about what happened. She entered the code into the door of our apartment and guided me in. I looked back to see Andrew but still couldn't make out anything but his Helly Hanson coat, jeans covering long legs and dark brown hair.

"Goodbye, Agent Bond. I hope you feel better." he said.

"Thanks for all your help, Andrew. Will I ever see you again, Andrew?" I said.

"I hope so." he said.

"My last name really is Bond you know."

"I know. Jennifer told me that that part wasn't the concussion talking. You got me." he said.

"I'll marry you one day if you want, Andrew. Then your last name can be Bond too. You'll get to be a secret agent." I said.

"That sounds great, Cassie. Looking forward to it. Goodbye." he said and walked down the hallway.

Chapter 2

CASSIE

"Did you know that the dot over a lowercase 'j' is called a 'tittle'?"

"I'll remember that the next time it comes up in conversation, Ruth."

Ruth, Jennifer, and I were standing in the middle of the campus green which was actually white with two-and-half-feet of new snow. I laid myself down into the snow to work on my snow angels. Saturdays would get pretty boring here in the winter so Ruth, Jennifer, and I decided to make snow angels and walk out large words in the snow on this sunny, snow covered, Saturday morning. Ruth wrote "Ruth and Jared" by meticulously walking out each letter. I just lazily waved my arms in the same snow angel I'd been making for four minutes.

It had been a week since my concussion and breakup with Jack so I was still a little out of sorts. Even though I was laying in feet of snow, it was still oddly loud. There were about five million people outside in the snow. I could hear shouting and screaming, snowball fights, and wrestling. I sighed loudly to indicate boredom but Ruth and Jennifer were perfecting their letters with their boots several yards away. They didn't hear me and I knew that they weren't bored yet. I was always bored. It was a fatal flaw of mine and I didn't know what to do to fix it at this particular moment.

"This is stupid and boring." I muttered aloud.

I reached into the snow and took a mouthful, refreshing myself with the cold sensation of the taste of winter in my mouth.

"Who are you talking to?" someone asked standing over me.

I couldn't make out what their face looked like with the bright sun glaring off of the snow, but I recognized the voice immediately.

"Andrew?" I said, wiping melted snow off of the side of my face and attempting to thaw out my now frozen mouth as I spoke.

"Hello." he replied with a small wave.

"How...how are you? I am so sorry. I didn't see you there. I wasn't really talking to anyone at all. My friends were right here but they walked away." I said awkwardly.

"I'm fine but I was actually wondering how you were doing. I was looking around campus all last week to see if you'd recovered but I never saw you until just now. Nice snow angel by the way."

He was smiling, genuinely happy to see me after admitting to searching for me all week long. My heart fluttered. I stood up to see him better and to not look like a crazy snow person.

"Thanks. It's my standard snow activity. I've been making them for years."

What a totally stupid thing to say.

"I think I'm recovered by the way. I had to skip all my classes and avoid screens this entire week. Potentially next week too. Thanks again for your help. I can't really remember much of what happened that night. My forehead is still pretty messed up." I said.

I took off my hat to reveal a purple and yellow bruise in the middle of my forehead.

As Andrew stepped closer to look at me, all of a sudden, I remembered everything about him. His light brown eyes and his interesting nose. He was wearing his same Helly Hanson coat but this time with a black winter hat. He was squinting in the bright winter sun but he looked even better in the daylight. I stepped a little closer to him as well so he could get a good look at my face. A look of concern and shock fell over his face as he squinted at my forehead.

I stood motionless as he silently continued to look me over. I wondered what he was thinking. *He would probably think I was pretty if it weren't for this embarrassing bruise. I should have stayed in my snow angel or at least left my hat on.*

"So, what do you think?" I asked.

I meant to ask him what he thought specifically of my bruise but I forgot half of the question.

"I think that's the worst bruise I've ever seen in my entire life and that I probably should have taken you to the ER last week." he admitted.

He looked mildly horrified and sounded earnest.

"Well, you did so much for me. I'm really, really grateful." I replied.

We stood in silence for another minute just staring at each other. It was odd but I didn't mind it.

"Do you want to go for a walk?" he asked suddenly.

Andrew seemed to surprise even himself when he asked the question.

"Sure." I said.

A walk in the winter day with this guy- don't mind if I do!

I prepared myself to be completely cured of boredom and hid my delight as I spotted Ruth and Jennifer. I yelled over toward them.

"I'm leaving! See you later!" I bellowed.

"Hold on!" yelled Jennifer.

"Who's that guy?" I heard Ruth loudly whisper to Jennifer as they walked in our direction.

"That's 'The Guy.'" Jennifer responded in an even louder whisper.

They had never looked more like ridiculous college girls as they approached Andrew and I with their frivolous scarves and brightly colored coats and boots. I felt a little mortified.

"Andrew, you remember Jennifer from last week. This is our other roommate: Ruth." I said.

"Hi Ruth. It's nice to meet you again, Jennifer." Andrew smiled.

I made a mental note of how impressed I was at his use of names.

"You too. Where are you guys going?" Jennifer asked with an unnecessarily wide grin.

"We're going for a walk; I'll be back later." I replied.

"Have fun! See you guys later!" Ruth exclaimed with way too much enthusiasm.

Ruth and Jennifer never thought much of Jack and were constantly annoyed by how much I had to run out of fun events to catch up with him on the phone. When Jennifer explained how good looking the guy who "rescued Cassie" was, they both lost their minds. *So mature.*

Andrew and I walked for at least a quarter of a mile before it felt like I had known him for my entire life. He was a great conversationalist and it never felt awkward even when we were silent for minutes at a time. I could tell he was genuinely interested in knowing me as a person and wasn't just taking pity on the clumsy girl with the giant bruise. We exchanged the basics of where we were each from, what we studied, and what our plans were after graduation.

"Do you have a job lined up already?" I asked.

"Yes, I actually have an internship at Madison and Williams and I'll be working there full time as soon as I graduate. What about you?" he said.

"Did you just say 'Madison and Williams'?" I asked.

"Yes, why?"

"I have a job lined up there...in public relations. That's my major." I was shocked.

Could this be real? I felt an inclination of a spark when I was dazed and confused from the telephone pole but now it felt like an actual lighter flicked on in between us as we walked on shoveled sidewalks. It was so coincidental that we would end up working at the exact same place in May.

"Are you serious? Madison and Williams? This is actually crazy." I whispered.

"I know! It is crazy." Andrew responded.

Is this real life? Is this destiny? Am I supposed to actually be with this guy?

"Andrew, can I ask you a serious question?" I asked.

I paused after I released the question into the wintery air.

"Sure. You can ask me anything, Cassie Bond..." he said, looking right at me.

"Do you think that rock climbing is stupid or do you think that it's cool? I know it's a weird question but I have to know your thoughts." I said.

I was putting him in the ultimate test. I always thought that rock climbing was so dumb and seemed so boring. After I broke up with Jack, I hated it more than ever. I had become so uninspired after hearing about it so much and knew for a fact I could never be with anyone who enjoyed it or even thought that it was a little bit cool.

Andrew turned his head to the side with a confused look at first, but then pondered the question, and answered me with confidence.

"I've never done it, so I can't say for sure how I feel. And I wouldn't want to judge something I hadn't tried, but to me: it looks really pointless." he said.

I couldn't have agreed more. His answer was more diplomatic than I would have liked but it worked for me. I began to daydream about making fun of rock climbers with Andrew as a proper adult in the future for a moment while I stood there looking at him. His face was perfect.

Every silly girl thought went through my mind. He stood facing me and took my hand. It felt completely natural and normal. We stood silently as we shared the same looks of wonder, amazement, and curiosity after sharing more details about our jobs awaiting us at the same exact company an hour away, near his hometown in the suburbs of Pittsburgh.

"It's a town called Sewickley. My family's lived there for generations. One day, I hope to raise a family there." he said, beaming at the thought of the future.

I could imagine it perfectly for him. For myself.

I thought for a moment he was going to kiss me, but instead, he gently tugged me along the sidewalk again. We floated along quietly for another few minutes until we came across a grove of snow-covered trees. We hadn't spoken in at least three entire minutes when he gently pulled me over to one of them. He slowly pressed me into the trunk and looked me up and down. Nothing was rushed but everything about the way he looked at me was impassioned.

Don't forget this moment. Don't forget the way he's looking at you. I slowed my breath as best as I could while under such close scrutiny. My eyes locked with his while I waited for him to lean in with his face. Instead, he reached out and touched either side of my face with both of his hands and stepped even closer. I felt the snow packed into the tree trunk behind me begin to soak through my hat but I didn't care. His hands were so warm, so big and slightly shaking. I felt him breathing. I felt his warm body pressing me further into the tree with his hips. He moved his hand right up to my hat, pulled it back a little, and carefully touched my bruise. Pressing his lips to it, he kissed me there, moved his lips down to my cheek, and inhaled the scent of my hair while pushing it away a little.

His mouth moved from my cheek up to my mouth. It was slow and fulfilling. His lips were warm and soft, he took his

time, and inhaled any ounce of air I had in my lungs. I took
the air right back and kissed him back harder. I felt him smile
as he kept kissing me. We embraced, kissing against the snow
covered tree for what felt like ages until I heard a snow plow
drive past. The harsh sound of the blade against the worn road
brought us both back into reality.

I stayed against the tree surrounded by Andrew's arms for
a few more minutes. For the first time in my life I felt at peace
without words of any kind. My ever-present urge to fill the
gaps of silent air wasn't forming in any way at all.

Andrew never took his eyes off of me while his hands
rubbed my arms up and down. He must have noticed the cold
more than I did because all I felt was warmth from the inside
out. I adored everything about that kiss, this moment, and the
fire I felt ignite in my chest.

*Is my concussion over now? Is this real? What am I even doing
right now?* I asked myself so many more questions while we
silently walked back toward campus. He walked me all the way
back to my apartment where he had so patiently waited with
me over a week ago. I had never felt so smitten by someone
this soon. We hardly knew each other but I knew he would
end up being someone I could soon hardly live without. When
we reached the door of my apartment, he kissed me again so
quietly and so tenderly, yet with so much passion. I knew I'd
marry him.

Chapter 3

CASSIE

It had been 11 months to the day since Andrew's accident. I didn't recognize myself from the person I was ten years ago, or the person I was ten months ago. So much had changed and so many things had happened. The amount of grief counseling that insurance will cover was mind-blowing. I met with my therapist Dr. Amdell weekly in the beginning and less and less until about a month ago. I could have stayed in that counselor's office for weeks straight and it wouldn't have mattered at all to my insurance agent.

"If you don't deal with your grief, your grief will deal with you, Cassie. Get it together and go over there." Jennifer told me over the phone more than once after the bustle of the funeral died down.

"I know. But if I go, I'll have to face reality on an even deeper level than I already am." I whined to her.

"Denial is a very dangerous thing, Cassie. Make the appointment." she lectured.

"OK I will."

I only agreed to go because the thought of Andrew still being alive after I had died, and then refusing to get help ruined me. I'd want him to heal, I'd want him to get better, and be able to function for the sake of our children. They deserved a parent who could be there for them in every way possible. After three weeks of crying in my bed, sitting on the couch for hours holding his wedding band in my hand, and staring into the empty air, I knew I needed to get it together. I wasn't myself and Jennifer was absolutely right. I put on my big girl pants, set his ring inside my jewelry box, and made the call.

I made the first appointment with Dr. Amdell and kept on going, sometimes with my small children and sometimes by myself for months. And it helped. It actually did. I was encouraged to try to find lessons in new experiences. I was back to work, back to reality, and making real progress in my new life as a single mother. I found moments where I could laugh without feeling guilty for it and I made it through some moments during the day where my thoughts weren't drifting to Andrew. It was hard but I was proud of myself for the work I had put in and the work I knew I could still put in.

New experiences equal new memories. I'll do it for myself and the kids. I'll make you proud, Dr. Amdell.

After six months, I found the courage to slip off my own rings one morning and set them in my jewelry box next to Andrew's ring and all of the other pieces he had given me over the years. I glanced at the necklace he bought me for our first anniversary. I gently touched the emerald earrings he bought me for my 30th birthday, and permitted myself to cry a little bit. I didn't wallow, I just let the tears come and go and I walked out of the room, no longer wearing the symbol of marriage around my left ring finger. It took me weeks to get used to the lighter feeling of my left hand, but I survived it, and was proud of myself again.

I noticed the calendar today and tried not to deny my sadness. I let it come and then pass on my way home from work. Today was a Wednesday which made me really motivated to get home. Andrew's parents lived locally and took my kids overnight every Wednesday so that I could have an evening to myself. I worked from home on Thursday's so it was a small vacation from single parenting in the middle of the week. It felt so good to walk through the door and be able to breathe a little bit. I arrived home and walked through the side door after getting the mail.

As I hit the lights on in the kitchen I dropped the mail on the counter. An envelope slid out of the center of the pile onto the floor. It didn't look like a standard bill envelope. It felt lighter and thinner as I picked it up to add it to the pile. I held it up to the light a little more. There wasn't a return address so I opened it quickly out of curiosity.

As I shoved my fingernail into the top of the envelope, I had a strange familiar feeling noticing the handwriting. I couldn't place whose it was but was sure I had seen it before.

DEAR CASSIE,

I WANTED TO EMAIL YOU BUT I ONLY HAD YOUR EMAIL ADDRESS FROM HIGH SCHOOL AND I DIDN'T THINK YOU STILL USED AGENTCASBOND@HOTMAIL ANYMORE. I HEARD ABOUT YOUR HUSBAND AND I CAN'T TELL YOU HOW SORRY I WAS TO HEAR ABOUT HIS DEATH. I NEVER MET HIM BUT HE HAD TO HAVE BEEN A PRETTY AMAZING GUY TO HAVE MARRIED

YOU. I'VE BEEN THINKING A LOT ABOUT WHAT YOU MUST HAVE GONE THROUGH AND I WANTED TO KNOW IF THERE IS ANYTHING I CAN DO TO HELP YOU AND YOUR CHILDREN.

LOVE,

Matt

What on earth is Matt Brooks doing sending me a letter? If he's still living upstate he must be at least six hours away...I haven't seen Matt in at least 15 years. How did he get this address?

I was so confused. Matt Brooks and I were acquaintances at our hometown high school in upstate New York. He was a senior when I was a junior and we had probably just two classes together. We had never dated or anything, and never had more than three deep conversations in total. We had passed a lot of very immature notes back and forth in a geometry class making fun of our teacher, but that was the extent of personal inter-action that merited any depth at all. Our parents didn't know each other at all either. How strange that he wanted to see me and seemed to feel so connected to me after all these years. I hadn't thought about Matt in ages and had absolutely no idea what kind of person he had become. *He could be a real creep...*

Creepy men had really made their way out of the wood-work this past handful of months. If there is something that almost everyone found attractive, it was death and grief. It became so uncomfortable that I actually had to disable my Facebook account. Men I hadn't spoken to in years were keen on messaging me about how much they'd love to help me through such a difficult time. I had actually convinced myself recently to get coffee with an old college friend of mine and Andrew's but about five minutes in, I realized we weren't there for sharing coffee and tears. It was clear that he wanted a lot more than caffeine as he lounged across the tiny high top table and attempted to kiss me. I slid off of my chair with disgusted surprise and made a promise to myself not to ever go "get coffee" with anyone again.

I wasn't ignorant to the fact that to the outside eye, death had some sort of odd aphrodisiac quality to it. At least many people around me seemed to feel this. I was still young, 31 years old, and in good shape considering I'd had two kids born just a year apart from each other. Now that Miles and Lydia were five and four, I no longer looked like a brand new mom who didn't have time to keep up with her appearance. Not being able to eat much of anything for months certainly contributed to my small waist and thin limbs. I kept my long blonde hair looking fresh in long waves and I paid decent attention to my skin. I had blue eyes and a big smile. My height was ideal for wearing heels without towering over people next to me. I had always loved high quality clothes but never dressed in a pretentious style, it was just classic. I was definitely considered good looking, but when Andrew entered a room, I felt like he was the real show-stopper. Maybe that was just me…

I went through the rest of my mail, took a hot bath, cried a little bit with a glass of wine, and went to bed. I longed for Andrew every night, especially when I was alone in the house. I never quite got used to the empty feeling of his side of the bed. I had caught myself talking to him in a state of half-sleep regularly. Even in the past weeks, it happened at least once each week.

When I woke up, I re-read the letter from Matt. It was kind of him to write to me. He was a really fun guy and definitely really nice. He certainly wasn't the type of guy to try to take advantage of my new situation. I felt optimistic as I sipped a cup of hot coffee in my office at home and began digging for the old cigar box I kept my stationary in. I had gone through more of my personal stationery in the past 11 months than I had in my entire life. So many people made us food, watched my kids, sent us flowers, and helped with the housework. It was overwhelming, and in a little bit of a sick sense, I was looking forward to being a year past Andrew's death. It seemed like the generosity of others slowed down more and more as a full year had neared and I was ready to be treated without pity by everyone around me.

I slid out a piece of light blue cardstock with my married name, "Cassie B. Caldwell", embossed at the top of it, and opened the drawer for one of my preferred letter-writing pens.

Dear Matt,

Thank you so much for your kind words and offer. It means so much that you reached out to me from so far away. Do you still live upstate? We had a lot of laughs in high school and I had fun recalling them after reading your letter. Also, you're right; I don't use that email address anymore. How embarrassing that would have been! I'm doing very well all things considered. Miles is 5 and Lydia is 4; they're both doing really well but it's definitely been an adjustment. Let me know if you want to get in touch sometime.

Agent Cassie Bond

I ended the letter with my phone number, sealed the envelope and held up my pen to write the address when I realized I didn't have one. How was I supposed to get this letter back to Matt? I guess I'd have to do a quick internet search. I sighed as I googled "Matthew Brooks". I hit enter and an absolute flood of articles, links, and pictures filled the computer screen of my office.

"Matthew Brooks Foundation","Matthew Brooks Medical Grant","Matthew Brooks Foundation to Build New Hospital Wing in Syracuse".

I was so confused; scrolling down the pages of articles, I clicked on no article or link in particular. The pictures were definitely of the Matt I once knew. He was tall, had an olive skin tone with darker blonde hair and bright blue eyes. I recalled his wide smile with his very bright white teeth. He looked like he kept himself in good shape with a lean frame and strong arms. There were pictures of him cutting ribbons in front of building sights, wearing a hard hat with a suit, and shaking hands with doctors. *Is he some sort of super-investor for hospitals?*

A million thoughts ran through my mind as I finally clicked on a link to his incredibly complex, yet somehow still vague website in an attempt to find his address. The only thing I could deduce from the website was that he was definitely some sort of benefactor or investor for large healthcare related projects. Building wings of hospitals, providing medical equipment to under-funded clinics, and the like. There wasn't any personal address given, but an address to a building in New York City. *I guess that's the address I'm using.*

I jotted down the address and set the letter under my keys. I only had a few minutes to pull myself together before meeting

Ruth for lunch. Jennifer didn't live nearby and sometimes was able to escape her new baby to join us about once every four or five times. Ruth ended up living 20 minutes away from me after she found a job at a top law firm in downtown Pittsburgh, but Jennifer was almost an hour away. I threw the letter in the mailbox with some bills on my way out of my neighborhood. Five minutes later, I slid across our normal booth at The Back Country Diner.

"It's 'Widow Wednesday!'" I heard Ruth proclaim as she walked through the door and approached the booth.

"Are we still using that term?" I asked.

"Of course we are!" she said.

Ruth was my height, had medium-length dark brown hair and usually wore it in a ponytail. She was in great shape and looked incredible today in her gray pantsuit. She really knew how to pull off the strong woman lawyer look which was the exact opposite of Jennifer's appearance. Jennifer had wild curly hair that wasn't quite brown and wasn't quite blonde. She dressed in maxi-dresses with giant floral patterns, and it wasn't weird to see her wearing gigantic earrings that completely distracted you from seeing her adorable, expressive face.

Ruth dumped about ten sugar packets on the table.

This diner was a little tricky in that it seemed like it was a greasy spoon sort of a place and even the name suggested it was standard diner food, but what was really going was that someone back in time decided that it should be "healthy" diner food. They mostly served a lot of horrible vegan dishes, but there were exactly four absolutely outstanding things on the menu that actually tasted great and made it worth going to. The girls and I rotated between the four items each week and decided to just bring our own sugar because crystalized agave just didn't cut it for sweetening our iced tea. The servers either didn't notice or didn't care. More than once, Ruth had also brought her own salad dressing in her large purse.

"Don't say it too loudly because it's actually Thursday and people will think we're crazy." I said.

"But I love the idea of confusing people so they miss their appointments thinking it's the wrong day and I love my little widow." she said, grabbing my face with both hands and squeezing my cheeks.

"I love you too Ruth, but maybe it's time for a new term."

"Widow Wednesdays" started about two months after Andrew died. His parents would pick up my kids from preschool and keep them overnight and for most of the next day. I had taken a leave of absence from work at the time and would have all of Wednesday to myself. In the beginning it was mostly to do things like meet with lawyers, banks, and insurance agents, but it turned into Ruth and Jennifer coming over in the evenings as much as they could for drinks and dinner with me so I wouldn't be alone as the sun went down. Jennifer cooked gorgeous meals and we stayed up late talking. It felt like a little taste of college life all over again in the middle of horrible things like work weeks and tragedy. Ruth started referring to them as "Widow Wednesday's" and the term stuck even when our get-togethers shifted to Thursday mornings after Jennifer had her baby about six months ago.

Ruth and I caught up for a few minutes while we waited for our sandwiches to come when I mentioned the letter from Matt.

"So listen to this: I got a letter from this dude I went to high school with yesterday." I said.

"Is that weird? I mean, weren't you getting like 20 of those a week for a while there?" she asked nonchalantly.

"I guess that's true. But this is weird because I haven't seen him in like 15 years and I never really knew him all that well to begin with. We had a few classes together but I really don't *know him*, know him." I explained.

"He sounds like a total weirdo." she said as she stirred another sugar packet into her iced tea.

"I googled him Ruth. Look at this." I said as I handed her my phone.

She scrolled through with an impressed and confused look on her face, her dark eyebrows expressive.

"Is he some sort of billionaire or something?" she asked.

"How should I know? He's obviously doing a bunch of nice things on a very, very large scale. The real question is what does he want with me? And the other real question is: how did he know about Andrew? We weren't even friends on Facebook."

"This is the greatest mystery of our time." Ruth replied flatly.

"Are you seriously not a little curious about this? You love stuff like this!"

"It just seems like another dude going for the grieving young mother, Cassie. It doesn't seem any different then any of those other creepers." she said.

"You have a point I guess. This one just seemed more intriguing than the others I guess. Oh well, I'm sure the address I used won't be right and he'll never get my thank you note anyway. How's work going?" I asked her, changing the subject entirely.

Almost an hour later as we stood up, I slugged down my

last sip of coffee out of the bright yellow, one-of-a-kind, hand-blown, artisan, clay mug and agreed to put the pressure on Jennifer to come next week. As I drove home, I couldn't take my mind off of Matt Brooks. No one else had bothered to write a handwritten letter. Everyone else our age had sent an email or a message online. *Matt kicked it old-school and I respect that.*

I always respected that. Andrew always did things like polish his shoes with shoe polish, grind his own coffee beans, and split all of our firewood by hand. He knew how to do everything the Right Way. It was so attractive and I didn't realize how attractive it was until he was gone. There wasn't anyone around to wax skis, plane doors, or make paper cranes. Andrew really knew how to do all those unique things that went beyond general handy husband skills. Every once in a while, I'd find a paper crane sitting on my pillow when I woke up. The kids would too. The look of delight on their faces when he was teaching them how to make paper cranes was better than Christmas morning to me. I adored watching their interest in how to make cranes. They were so quiet and so still while they watched Andrew's fingers fold and bend the tiny squares of paper as he patiently explained what he was doing. They never took their eyes off of his hands and even when he slowed down so they could try to follow along, they never could quite get it.

I kept an old shoebox filled with dozens of poorly made cranes made by Miles and Lydia with dozens of perfectly made cranes made by Andrew. They were all different colors, the kids had even colored on some of the cranes; the inside of the box is gorgeous with the combination of textures and colors. I told myself that if my house was ever on fire, that shoebox would be the first item I would grab.

I arrived home and headed to my office to get some work done. I became bored of work after an hour and just for fun, I logged onto Hotmail. It took me five attempts to remember my password from high school, but I finally got into my old email account. When I scrolled through the emails, I had to laugh at first. There were hundreds of unopened emails, mostly spam emails for makeup products, restaurant coupons, party supplies, and wholesale candle wick sale coupons. I found a few random emails from my mother who would send inspirational quotes accompanied by videos of blooming flowers exploding glitter. She sent Bible verses, daily devotionals, and book recommendations that her best friend Jeanie says, "you have to read ASAP!". It wasn't unlike the emails she still sent me now. Some things never changed.

I kept scrolling down where I found a few emails with Matt's old email address he used in high school. There were a few from our back and forth about a geometry project we were assigned as partners for. We had to draw a city together using protractors, compasses, and other geometric tools I paid no attention to. It was fun because Matt did most of the work.

School, like most things, really bored me so my contribution was making jokes about phallic-shaped buildings. Our email exchanges were only about when we should meet up to draw our final city. We agreed to meet at the local library because it was walking distance for both of us. We met there, Matt drew the city, we laughed, turned in the project the next day, and never had much interaction after that because he graduated and went to college out of state at Ault College in Illinois on an impressive academic scholarship. I didn't know the details because I didn't pay close attention, but I remembered that he was beyond smart and had a really genuine personality that would definitely have shown during a college interview.

I kept scrolling through emails from his address. I found more than I remembered and was taken aback when I saw that there were at least ten that were unread.

One was from right after our geometry project.

```
5:05pm
FROM: mbrooks@aultcollege.edu
TO: agentcasbond@hotmail.com
SUBJECT: none


Hey Cassie,
    I just wanted to tell you that I really en-
joyed working on that final with you. I haven't
laughed like that in a few months so thanks.
    Matt
```

The next one was from almost a year later.

```
4:15pm
FROM: mbrooks@aultcollege.edu
TO: agentcasbond@hotmail.com
SUBJECT: Hang out?


Hey Cassie,
    I know it's been a while but I wondered how
```

your senior year was going? I'm at college for
now but I'll probably be back in town soon. My
mom is sick so I might have to drop out. Let me
know if you want to get together anytime.
    Matt

The next one was from only a month after that one.

11:45am
FROM: mbrooks@aultcollege.edu
TO: agentcasbond@hotmail.com
SUBJECT: none

Hey Cassie,
    You probably aren't using this email ad-
dress anymore so you probably won't get this
but I figured I'd let you know that I actually am not in town anymore the way I thought
I would be. My mom died from cancer about two
weeks ago and I'm moving out West. My dad decided he didn't want to stay in the house so
he just listed it and found a place out there.
I'm bummed we never got to hang out again but I
hope you're doing well and let me know if you
get this.
    Matt

He was right, I had stopped using that email address. Once Facebook came out, I basically never used my high school email again. I went off to college and was given a new one by the school. I kept reading the next emails.

9:56pm
FROM: matthewbrooks@statecollegeofcol.edu
TO: agentcasbond@hotmail.com
SUBJECT: none

Hey Cassie,

I know for a fact you are definitely not using this email address because you've never responded but it really helps me to feel like I have someone to communicate with. It's been six months since my mom died and I really haven't been doing all that well. I feel so stupid writing this and now I sort of hope you never use this email again, but I feel like I'm drowning all the time. My dad just constantly works and the new college I'm going to is so much bigger than Ault was. I really liked going to Ault and now I'll never get to go again. I haven't gotten to know anyone out here. I miss my mom, I miss Ault, I miss home, and I miss laughing. I feel like I haven't laughed in ages. You really knew how to make me laugh and I wanted to thank you for that, Cassie. You were always a lot of fun. I never got to know you the way I wanted to and

I know we don't know each other that well but
if you ever do read this, I want you to know
that you are helping me through a really hard
time without even knowing it. Thanks, Cassie.

Matt

The next one was written months later.

1:32am
FROM: matthewbrooks@statecollegeofcol.edu
TO: agentcasbond@hotmail.com
SUBJECT: none

Cassie,
    It's been a year since I lost my mom and
I'm really not doing much better than I was
months ago. I really need someone to talk to.
My classes are going fine and my roommate is
cool but I just haven't laughed in so long and
I don't know if I ever will again. I really
need to laugh again. I just don't know how to.

Two months later.

1:12am
FROM: matthewbrooks@statecollegeofcol.edu
TO: agentcasbond@hotmail.com
SUBJECT: none

Cassie,

I know you aren't reading these but I just
had to tell you that I feel really stupid sending that last email. I've thought about it ev-
eryday and I wish I wasn't sending you these.
If you ever see all these, just delete them. I'm
not a crazy person and I know I sound like one.
Some grief counselor told me that I have 'situ-
ational depression'... I think I'll be fine. I
seriously hope you haven't read these.

A year later.

11:04pm
FROM: matthewbrooks@statecollegeofcol.edu
TO: agentcasbond@hotmail.com
SUBJECT: none

Hey Cassie,

I'm only writing this because I know for
sure there's no chance you read these or would
ever use this email. You are probably in college
and would never use this one. I'm doing a lot

better. I only have a few semesters left here
at college and I have made a few really awesome friends. It's been really helpful to me and
I'm actually having some fun out here. I didn't
think Colorado would ever grow on me but I think
it has. I can think so clearly at the top of a
giant rock. I can see for miles and the air is
so fresh up there. My one friend taught me how
to rock climb and I actually do it every single day now. I remember when you used to make
fun of surfers and did that hilarious impression of a stoned surfer in the middle of class
and I imagine you'd do a similar impression for
rock-climbers but I promise they aren't all bad.
The clarity of mind is unreal and I think I've
been able to process more about my mom's death
than I ever have before. I miss her so much and
I feel really cheesy saying that. You would
definitely make fun of me if you met me now.
Cassie, I still think about you sometimes. I really do. I know it sounds crazy but when I think
about you it really relaxes me and it makes me
feel so calm. I feel so dumb typing this. I like
you a lot Cassie, and I know you're still as
cool as you were a few years ago. Please never
change no matter what happens.

  Matt

Three months later.

3:14am
FROM: matthewbrooks@statecollegeofcol.edu
TO: agentcasbond@hotmail.com
SUBJECT: I saw you!

Cassie!
I saw you! I was back home and I saw you! I am actually kicking myself for not stopping the car and flagging you down but I wasn't sure it was you until it was too late. I was back in town for John Robert's birthday weekend and I saw you at a gas station filling up your tank while I was at that intersection near Tires Plus and The Flower Diner. I can't believe it was you. Did you go to that party? You must be home for Summer Break? You look exactly the same! I'm so sorry I didn't say hello. I actually can't believe how much I'm regretting it. I hope you're doing really well. I think about you all the time. You're really cool and I hope you always know that.
Matt

Four years later!

9:54am
FROM: m.brooks@pfizernyc.com
TO: agentcasbond@hotmail.com
SUBJECT: none

Cassie.

It's been so long since I've written to you but I was sending a work email and there's someone named Cassandra in the list of emails I had to send and as I started typing the name, your email came up automatically. It's been so long and I don't even know what to say. I've been done with college for years now and I'm living in New York City. I actually do hate it. It's nothing like upstate where we grew up. I hate the noise and I hate how busy it is. I work in the medical field. You would think it was so boring. You found a lot of things boring and I know that if I explained my office job to you that you would lose interest immediately. What else is new? Well, I haven't been rock climbing in a few years. That's depressing. I was re-reading some of the old emails I sent you and I can't believe how often I used to climb. I'm so sorry if you've ever read all these. My friends still go all the time but I never do. I can't imagine how I'd go now living in the city and being so busy with work. Did I mention I hate it so much? Cassie, I hope you are doing well. I haven't seen you in years and I'm try-

ing to imagine what you look like. Is your hair
still blonde? Do you wear glasses now? Are you
married? Do you have kids? I am none of those
things except my hair still is blonde. I wish
it wasn't a lot of the time. Do you know how
hard it was to be taken seriously while trying
to sell medical supplies with blonde hair and a
rock-climbing tan right out of college? No one
took me seriously and everyone thought I was
a lifeguard stoner. Even the suits didn't help
at first. I can only imagine what your life is
like. I hope your family is doing well. Mine
isn't. My dad is in poor health so he moved back
upstate. I have to go back there all the time
to help him. It's difficult because I'm so far
away in NYC and did I mention that I just absolutely loathe it? Did I mention that it's super
noisy and you can't sleep at night? It's true
what that song says. This city and the people
in it literally never sleep. I'm tired. I would
do anything to be back in my hometown, back in
my bed with the plaid sheets my mom bought me
sleeping until 10am on a Saturday. Adulthood
isn't as much fun as I knew it wouldn't be.
Wouldn't it be crazy if you actually had been
reading all of these emails for all these years?
One can dream...or dread!

    Matt

The latest email was written just a few weeks ago.

5:57pm
FROM: matt.brooks@tmbf.com
TO: agentcasbond@hotmail.com
SUBJECT: none

My Dearest Cassie,
   I don't even know what to say. I am so, so
sorry to hear about your husband's death. I
know we haven't seen each other in years but I
heard about it from a friend and I had to say
something even though I know you probably won't
get this. I can't explain why but I truly have
thought about you regularly for the past fifteen
years. You really don't deserve to go through
this kind of grief. Cassie I hope you're hanging in there. I don't live in New York anymore.
My dad passed away recently so I've been trying
to handle all of that and I'm in the process of
taking my entire company to Pittsburgh. I know
you don't live far from there. I'm going to
write you a letter. This email isn't enough and
if I'm being honest with myself, I'd rather just
talk to you in person. I miss familiar faces so
much and you'd be like a small piece of home and
old times if I could just see your face for five
minutes. I doubt you feel the same way but I
hope if I write you a letter you'll know someone

from your past is rooting for you. I'm going to
write to you now Cassie.
　Love, Matt

I sat at my desk chair stunned and shocked. Matt had been writing to me for years and I had no clue. I had been through a whirlwind of emotions reading his old emails and didn't quite know what to think. He was living so close to me now. How was this possible after all these years? I felt very desperate for Matt to get my thank you note now. It would probably never make it to him. That address I sent it to was in New York City. He wasn't even living there anymore.

　I pulled my chair closer to the computer, clicked once again on his latest email and hit "reply".

Chapter 4

MATT

I almost fell out of the desk chair in my new office when I saw I had received an email from agentcasbond@hotmail again for the first time in 15 years. Sitting in front of my computer with my keyboard beneath my shaking hands, I clicked the email open and tried to pace my breathing. I could hardly see straight as my eyes crashed upon her words and about one million thoughts raced through my mind.

```
1:44pm
FROM: agentcasbond@hotmail.com
TO: matt.brooks@tmbf.com
SUBJECT: Hello

Dear Matt.
```

I don't quite know what to say or how to respond. Firstly, I'd like to thank you for your condolences about my husband. It was unexpected in the absolute worst way I never could have possibly imagined. It has taken me months to even write or say his name without falling to pieces on my kitchen floor, crumble into a ball onto my bed, or share moments with my children without hiding tears behind my sunglasses. It has been soul-crushing and excruciating for almost a year now and I really, really feel touched by your words of encouragement. I am on the mend and will be fine in time.

My kids are well and have impressed me with how easily they have adapted to new situations and still cherish memories of their father. Telling them about the accident was the worst moment of my life and even typing about it has me reliving it in ways I do not care to.

I can't believe you're moving to Pittsburgh, Matt. It's so close to me and I'm there all the time! I sincerely hope you like it better than you liked New York. Speaking of New York: it is the perfect segway to tell you now that I did, just now, read all your emails from years ago. Remind me never to live in New York City. I knew I always hated that place. It sounds like you absolutely loved it... I wish you had called me or something; I had no idea I'd made such an impression on you in high school. I'm really glad that you found a

way to process your mother's death even if it was
doing the one thing in life I know I'd absolutely hate: rock climbing. Are you in a fraternity or
is it just assumed men in their 20's and 30's all
do completely cliche activities out there? Do you
and your rock climbing friends all call each other, 'brah'? Do you have rock climbing lingo that
sounds as stupid as surfers lingo? Enlighten me.

But seriously, I'm really sorry, it sounded really painful. And I'm also sorry to see that your
dad has also passed away. Death, am I right? It's
the gift that just keeps giving these days. It's
so fun!

Let's get in touch if you still want to. I know
you might be in the process of moving but I have
every Wednesday evening and Thursday available for
coffee or whatever you'd like.

Cassie. Cassie Bond. Agent Cassie Bond.

Well actually it's Cassie Caldwell, but
whatever.

I dropped my head in my hands and looked down at my
shoes. I can't believe what I had just read. Cassie wanted to get
together. She had read all those emails. All those stupid emails
from college. I was so embarrassed I could hardly think straight.
Simultaneously, both my worst fear and biggest dream were both
happening at the same time. I laughed nervously out loud at her
jokes about rock climbing and at the notion of actually meeting
her in person again.

Cassie was known in high school as a total class clown but she wasn't the obnoxious kind. She was genuinely funny and just wanted to do anything other than school. It actually seemed pretty crazy and surprising to most people that she even bothered going to college because her aversion to anything academic was made very clear to fellow students, teachers, and administrators alike. She didn't seem to care much for sports either though. It was like anything school-related repulsed her. She spent her after school hours running an actual business of making and selling candles to any and every gift shop or spa in the area. She even paid local taxes on what she made. She was entrepreneurially-minded even at 16. Evidently, it's what paid for her college tuition according to some mutual friends.

Once I had overheard her try to bargain with the biology teacher while I was roaming the halls during a study hall period.

"Why don't I just show you how I 'use science' when I make this lavender blasted lemon sunshine candle instead of dissecting the worm, Mr. Carpet?"

"That's not science and it won't count as the same thing Ms. Bond."

"Are you sure, Mr. Carpet?" she asked. "It really is scientific what I'm doing. You have to measure the right amount of oil and lemon rinds and stuff. Then you mix it with the wax..."

"That's basic math, Ms. Bond. Not biology."

"I can offer you a written paper on biology after my date with Johnny if that's what you're after, Mr. Carpet." she winked as she retorted.

"Office. Now."

"OK, OK, I'll dissect the worm. Geez oh man, Mr. Carpet." she said.

She got detention.

She was something else back then and just from reading her email I could tell she was just as fun now. She had a confidence about her I just couldn't work out in my head. What was I supposed to say in response to this email? She had been through so much recently and I didn't want to jump headfirst into her life if she didn't actually want that. She could have just been being polite when she offered getting together. She probably thought I was the most pathetic person.

I had nothing to offer someone as incredible as Cassie. I didn't have any sort of notion of parenting having been an only child and I rarely interacted with kids on a personal level at all. My friend Juan's kids were the only children I ever had any sort of connection with and could deduce the concept of parenting from. She had two small children and had been married for years. Her life was so different from mine. Until now, I had really only been in a few semi-serious relationships. I had just ended things with a girl from New York who I saw no future with. I had yet to find someone who I thought I could really go all-in with. I also had my doubts about women's intentions with me as soon as the Matthew Brooks Foundation gained public attention.

It was just a random pairing that had Cassie and I working together on a math project and since then I'd been a silent observer and fan of her from afar. It was a really fun two weeks for me and the impression Cassie left on me after getting to know her on a personal level was very unexpected. She was fiery and jabbed me in all the right ways. She also had a warm and encouraging way about her; it was something I never completely figured out. She was the most intriguing combination of personalities.

Well here goes nothing. I hit the reply button and started typing.

2:12pm
FROM: matt.brooks@tmbf.com
TO: agentcasbond@hotmail.com
SUBJECT: hello back

Cassie.
I'm not sure what to say other than I'm just
really, really sorry about all those emails…

I didn't know how to continue this email. Every other time,
when it was clear to me that she wasn't even using this email
account, the words just came to me and I had no issue, no
mental block on what to say. Feelings just flowed out of me. So
much had happened and I was different now; I didn't have the
best read on my own emotions but I knew I wanted to see her
if she wanted to see me. I ran my hands through my hair and
continued typing after a few moments.

I look back on my college years and see that
I was going through a lot. I had a lot to process and sending you emails was a good outlet
for me. It worked for me at the time and I'm
really sorry if those caught you off-guard. I
promise I am no longer a depressed twenty-some-
thing. It sounds like it has been quite the
year for you. I'd love to get together for coffee sometime and Thursday mornings are great
for me. I'm actually completely moved now; my

business isn't all the way settled but I am. I
am happy to report that I can sleep in this city
and I don't hate it. It's hard to hate Pittsburgh when you compare it to New York.

　　Love, Matt

I hit send without proof-reading the email in case I chick-
ened out. Minutes later she replied.

2:20pm
FROM: agentcasbond@hotmail.com
TO: matt.brooks@tmbf.com
SUBJECT: hello back back

Dear Matt,
　　Pittsburgh>any other city. Big facts. Let's
meet at this place I've tried a few times near
where I live in Sewickley. It's called The Other
Diner. Can you do 9:30am?
　　Also, I'm glad to hear that you are on the
other side of your delayed teenage angst. I
think I'm getting close to being through mine.
Time will tell. Maybe just as I'm done with
mine, my kids will step into theirs??? So that
gives me, what? Another ten years of this?
Should be a fun ride for sure.
　　See you on Thursday morning!
　　Agent Bond

All of a sudden I felt like I only had one week to get my entire life pulled together. I looked to the left and to the right of me in a small panic. My apartment was messy and covered with half-opened boxes. Dishes weren't completely set away in the kitchen and the counter was completely covered with them. My clothes were strewn all over the bedroom and the living room had the most unopened boxes of all.

She's not coming here, relax. I told myself.

I still felt the need to get it together; that's the kind of effect Cassie had on people. She had high standards for herself and everyone around her. It never came off as mean though, always just as what was expected. I stood up and started toward the kitchen. I had never given so much thought to where dishes should go in my entire life. I had lived in plenty of random apartments and houses and had moved countless times but I never wracked my brain about the best way to set it up and unpack as I had today. This move had an effect on me and the thought of seeing Cassie after all these years had an even bigger effect on me. Time to get organized.

Chapter 5

CASSIE

"I don't want to excite you Mom, but I'm getting coffee with someone tomorrow. Do you remember Matt Brooks from high school? He was a year older than me? It's not a date by the way."

I was on the phone with my mom on the way home from work on Wednesday. It was pouring rain so I was relieved when I got off of the bigger roads and continued down the winding, pretty back roads closer to home. I'd never loved the weather in western Pennsylvania much.

"That's great!" she shouted a little too quickly.

She was slightly obsessed with the thought of me being in another marriage. She and many of her Baby-Boomer-aged friends could not understand how I could possibly live my life without a husband and even though she and my dad adored Andrew, he was total history to her now that she was finished grieving. Nothing would excite her more than me re-marrying.

"Mom, please don't get too excited about this and you didn't even answer my other questions. Do you remember him at all? Did you ever know his parents?" I asked.

"No, Honey. Never heard of them. What does he look like? Does he have a good job? Where are you meeting him? Does he live close to you?"

She kept asking questions and I immediately regretted even telling her about seeing him tomorrow.

I answered almost all of her questions, changed the subject, and hung up. Once I walked inside the house, I entered what I thought was blissful silence. *Maybe this isn't blissful. It's so quiet. Maybe Widow Wednesday's need to be back on actual Wednesday's again…*

I was a little lonely on these Wednesday nights lately. The kids were a great distraction from my thoughts in the evenings when I picked them up and they went on about their craft projects at preschool and played together or had me painting their faces and singing songs.

What should I do with myself tonight?

I slipped out of my work pants and heels and reached for my long burgundy henley top and black leggings. I pulled my long blonde hair into a messy bun and thought about what I should do next. All the bills were paid and the house was clean. I was at total loose ends, something that almost never happened. I had been putting off going through the last of Andrew's things so maybe this was the time to do it. I walked into the kitchen and tried not to think too hard about the task ahead. I made myself a Whiskey Sour and headed up the stairs. I flung open the door to his closet in our bedroom. We each had our own which was a major selling point when we bought the house.

I can do this. I can do this.

As I hit the lightswitch my eyes clouded with tears. I had made several attempts at going through his clothes over the past 11 months, but never could make a real move. Everything was just as he left it. We had installed a fancy closet system in both our closets shortly after we bought the house. Andrew's closet was impeccably orderly and it smelled slightly of cedar combined with his cologne: it smelled like heaven. His jeans were folded neatly, his shirts hung by category. Work pants hung neatly on one side and suits were hung toward the back of the closet. On the right side there were drawers of socks, boxers, and T-shirts. His sweaters were folded on the top shelf. The only thing out of place were his shoes; it was clear he had been trying on several pairs the morning of the accident and didn't have time to put the pairs he decided against away on the lower shelf.

Tears ran down my face as I touched almost every single piece of clothing in the closet. In a way it felt like touching him. The smell of the closet, the feeling of the folded wool sweaters, and the taste of the bourbon brought back so many memories. I closed my eyes and just stood there motionless for what felt like hours, just remembering. I could imagine Andrew standing in the closet with me telling me about his day, holding me in his strong arms, or kissing me. I could almost feel him breathing and taste his lips. I imagined his face brushing against mine as his arms slid around my waist. His voice whispering in my ear, telling me he loved me, his mouth trailing across the side of my neck, over the side of my face to my chin, and up to my mouth. He tasted like bourbon, his lips pressed my mouth open, and he moved his tongue inside, forcing mine open wider.

I gasped at my imagination and forced myself back to reality. I hit the light off, closed the closet door, and walked back downstairs. I was mad at myself and felt full of regret for ever going in the closet at all. *I can't do this now. As it turns out, Cassie, you're weak. Get yourself together.*

I avoided even going upstairs to the bedroom for the rest of the night. When I finally did go back upstairs to bed I didn't even look in the same direction as the closet.

The next morning I remembered that I had cancelled "Widow Wednesday" with Ruth to meet up with Matt. Jennifer wasn't able to come this direction anyway. I was a little anxious to meet up with Matt again after so many years and I was still a little distracted by my attempt at Andrew's closet from the night before. I fought off feelings of anger with myself as I began to get ready. His death was stinging this morning and I really wasn't myself. The combination of nerves and grief was making me cranky. I didn't have the guts to actually call Matt on the phone and cancel, plus I knew if I got out of the house I would be distracted from my mood. I had to get out of this house and as far away from Andrew's closet as possible. It felt like a sin to think about taking even a sock out of it.

I showered, dressed in jeans, and a new light blue blouse with bright red flats when I caught a glance of the rain that was still pouring outside. Rain boots would make more sense for going across parking lots today but I didn't want to look totally casual. I kept the red flats on and grabbed my red raincoat and purse and headed out to my car. I scrambled for the lipstick that lived in my center console as I drove closer to the diner.

I didn't suggest The Back Country Diner for a few reasons. Firstly, it was a sacred place for "Widow Wednesdays" with Ruth and Jennifer, and secondly, I really didn't think it would be appropriate to pull sugar packets out of my purse in front of Matt. He really didn't know me that well and I didn't need him to know that side of me at this point in time.

I parked in front of The Other Diner. It was actually called The Other Diner, but it also happened to be "the other diner" in town. It was sandwiched between a high-end gift shop and a nail salon in an upscale plaza. *He doesn't need to know how ridiculous this town can be…*

I took a deep breath and tried to calm my nerves as I pulled my hood over my hair to keep it dry and walked toward the diner. As I got closer I saw a line of people coming out of the opened front glass doors of the diner. *A line to get in on a Thursday morning? What's going on?*

There was no sign of Matt as I walked closer but there was a cloud of smoke and quite a bit of commotion.

"What the hell is going on here?" I asked a random middle-aged woman who was standing on the sidewalk in front of the diner.

"The kitchen just caught on fire. They made everyone evacuate but it might be OK to go back inside in a few minutes." she said as though a fire was a completely normal event to happen in a restaurant.

"Are you kidding me? A fire? Why would you want to go back inside with all that smoke? Is that seriously what people are waiting for in this line?" I asked, completely shocked.

She shrugged at me.

"The manager said everyone would get to eat for free if it cleared up and if we waited for a while. The fire marshall said maybe 45 minutes until it's all cleared away." she explained.

I was appalled.

"'Eat for free'? That's the most insane thing I've ever heard in my entire life. There is smoke literally BILLOWING out of the front door of this diner! Do you have an idea how badly your clothes and hair are going to smell after walking back into a restaurant that's had a grease fire in a disgusting dirty kitchen? Are the omelettes here really worth it?" I said, basically shouting, as I tried to back away.

This woman was clearly out of her mind and now I hated The Other Diner.

"Well excuse me, Honey! Not everyone can afford to eat breakfast at Starbucks!" she exclaimed.

"Starbucks? Who's going to Starbucks to eat breakfast? It's for a coffee on the run. That's why there's a drive-through. Furthermore, this is a fairly affluent neighborhood my friend; you'd be hard-pressed to find anyone who 'can't afford Starbucks'. The food here is the highest priced in the area. This really is 'the other freaking diner'...what a joke! They should shut the doors, close for the day, and take the hit! I can't believe how unprofessional this is!"

I was fuming mad. *So much for proving this town isn't completely ridiculous. Not only are the diners on fire, but the people are insane.*

I was about to open my mouth to continue to belittle The Other Diner to no one in particular when I saw a tall man in jeans and a raincoat approaching.

An actual raincoat. Not an absorbent jacket. I'll be damned. A real man who dresses for the weather.

"Matt?" I asked through the rain, praying that he didn't see my interaction with the woman on the sidewalk.

"Cassie!" he responded, his beautiful teeth beaming into a huge smile.

Before I could open my mouth to speak again he had pulled me into a giant hug. I didn't even get a good look at his face before he was bringing me into his arms and chest. He smelled like expensive, familiar cologne and laundry detergent. Raindrops bounced off of his jacket next to my face while we hugged. *The perfect repellent fabric for rainfall. He gets it.*

"Nice raincoat!" was all I could think to say as we hugged.

"Thanks!" he said.

We broke apart and stepped back a bit. As I gave him a once over, I again became very aware of the fact that I had just been yelling at a stranger as he was approaching. If he heard me, he probably thought I was totally crazy. I pushed down the embarrassment of what had just happened and continued touring him with my eyes.

Matt was beyond handsome. He had perfect short, blonde hair almost exactly the same color as mine. His eyes were still so blue, almost the same color as mine, and he was Andrew's exact height. His olive skin looked healthy and glowed, even on such a cloudy day. He had to have grown at least six inches since high school because I didn't remember him being this tall. I could tell he kept himself in good shape even though I assumed he didn't still go rock-climbing. He was a year older than me but his face looked just the slightest bit more worn, he looked more like three years older than me. His raincoat was navy blue and his jeans looked brand new. I wondered what he thought about my appearance as I noticed his eyes giving me a once-over.

"Do we look like siblings or am I crazy?" I asked, smiling at the notion.

"I think we do look a little bit alike!" Matt admitted with a laugh.

I decided to change the subject from our appearances to the current restaurant situation.

"So I hate to break it to you, but this piece of garbage diner has had a fire according to the people on the sidewalk and I don't think we can go here." I told him.

"Umm...OK." he looked confused, his eyebrows raised.

"I didn't plan this, I promise. I've only been here twice in my life and I've lived in this town for almost ten years. I usually go to this other place down the road." I explained.

"Should we go there instead?" he asked.

"Umm. I don't think so. I. I don't want to go there." I replied, trying not to hide the change in my tone of voice.

"OK."

He looked confused but agreeable.

"We can go to my house for coffee."

I blurted out the words before I even knew what I was saying. They just fell out of my mouth like it was the most natural thing in the world to invite someone I barely knew over to my empty house in the middle of a Thursday.

"Are you sure?" Matt asked with a slightly surprised expression.

"Umm yeah, why not? My kids aren't home so it's quiet there and I have a coffee maker."

What am I saying? What am I doing?

"OK, should I just follow you or...?" he asked.

"Yes! That's perfect!" I said with way too much enthusiasm.

We exchanged small talk about the area and the distance

between my house and the diner while we walked across the parking lot. My flats were soaking wet and my brain felt like it had fallen out of my skull. I was majorly regretting not bringing an umbrella like a real grown-up as raindrops still spat out of the gray sky. I had this morning so well planned and it was continuing to go sideways. Now I had to pray that my house wasn't completely destroyed with toys, dishes, and papers when I walked through the front door with a stranger I invited over without thinking.

I nervously drove down the wet, winding roads to my house as Matt followed me in his brand-new looking car. I wondered what Matt would think of my house and what he would think of me in general as we pulled into my driveway.

I inhaled and tried to shake off the strange feelings that took over me as I realized this was the first time I'd brought a man back to the house Andrew and I shared together as a married couple. I wasn't married anymore, but it felt a little bit wrong. I knew it wasn't a betrayal in my head, but my heart was doing weird things inside my chest.

My driveway was about a quarter of a mile long with apple trees lining the entire length of it on both sides. The house was a historic brick colonial that had a significant amount of renovations before Andrew and I bought it two years after we were married. I was pregnant with Miles and we needed more space. Our double income really helped allow us to upgrade at a young age. We didn't skimp on our own renovations and now I felt a little embarrassed at the size and grandeur of my house as Matt followed me to the front of the garage. I didn't open the garage door to pull into it in case it was a mess, and parked outside of the right side door. I was already soaking wet so what was the difference if I walked all the way to the front door instead of through the coverage of the garage.

My chest felt tight and I was oddly aware of my hair as Matt opened his driver door and stood. He seemed to have grown another few inches in stature on the drive over. He appeared even taller now that he was in my driveway.

"We can go through the front door over here." I yelled over the sheets of rain.

He nodded and followed me up the flagstone path.

I was too busy unlocking the large door handle and deadbolt to notice the package to my left. Matt reached down and picked it up for me.

"Thanks." I replied, not considering how heavy it could have been for him to hold.

I once again forgot how to form words as we walked inside. Matt held the package as we went through to the kitchen. It looked light and I remembered the new books and soccer balls I had ordered for Miles and Lydia and was glad it wasn't heavy after all. I had no idea what to do next. I hadn't been this nervous in a really long time and now I didn't have the stupid Other Diner as a safety net. I had brought Matt right into the eye of the hurricane by bringing him here.

Would he expect me to give him a full tour of my house? Would it be rude if I didn't? What was normal? Do I lead him around each room explaining all of the upgrades and changes my dead husband and I had made to each one over the over eight years we were married? Was I supposed to take him upstairs? It would feel so scandalous to show him where I slept, the bedroom where Andrew and I used to sleep, dream, get dressed, and have sex. It seemed like an absolutely outrageous idea.

Nothing felt normal and my thoughts were confusing me. I slowly walked toward the kitchen knowing that if I started a pot of coffee it would give me time to collect myself and catch my breath.

"I love old houses. It looks like you've done a really good job renovating this one." Matt said.

He set the package on the kitchen table which luckily had been perfectly clean. The rest of the house passed as well. I exhaled and looked at him. He went on about how great it looked while he took off his raincoat and hung it behind one of the kitchen table chairs. I took this as a sign to keep things in the kitchen, tentatively taking off my coat and hanging it on the back of the chair across from his.

He intently admired Miles and Lydia's pictures on the fridge and smiled not knowing I was watching him as I pulled two mugs out of the cabinet above the coffee maker. I set the mugs down near the coffee as it dripped out, releasing the smell of hazelnut.

"Do you take cream or sugar?" I asked.

"I drink it black." he replied. *Thank God.*

"I hope it's OK that we are at my house. I had high hopes for the diner. I'm so sorry." I said.

"Don't apologize. I love seeing where you live. I haven't even asked you how you are Cassie, I'm the one who should be apologizing." he said.

"Oh. Don't apologize. Here's your coffee. We can sit down here."

I gestured to the table and we sat down facing each other.

"To answer your question: I am doing well. It took a while to get my bearings but here I am." I said, settling into my chair and gripping my coffee with both hands.

"Cassie. I do have to apologize to you. I feel like I just threw myself into your life without you even asking me. Please tell me if I'm catching you off-guard by even communicating with you. I really feel like I cannonballed you and I feel like I'll never live down those emails." he said, looking sincere.

"If you say you're sorry to me one more time, I'm going to scream. Since last week I think I've either read the words 'I'm sorry', or heard you say them to me about 20 times. Stop apologizing. You didn't just bomb into my life. I liked reading your letter and your emails from all those years ago. We had fun in high school, didn't we? Why should this be weird?" I asked.

I was asking myself the last question as much as I was asking him.

"You're right. I won't apologize anymore. I'm sorry." he said.

"Seriously?" I said with a raised eyebrow.

"It's been a weird time with moving and everything." he replied.

"Are you here all alone? No family out here or anything?" I asked.

I felt more settled as Matt began to answer.

"Not a soul. I needed a fresh start after my dad died and I essentially have no family. I'm an only child and I don't have any living aunts and uncles I'm close with. After my dad, I decided to make some big changes. I broke up with a girl I had been seeing casually, I made big changes to my business, and found the perfect place to set it up where it would still function the way it always has but that wasn't New York. I hate that place so much." he explained.

"What exactly do you do for work?" I asked.

I discreetly slipped my soaking wet shoes off under the table and brought my knees close to my face, leaning forward while he spoke. I listened intently.

"It's a little hard to explain but basically after I saw how out of date the hospital was when my mom was dying of cancer years ago, it changed my entire life. I intentionally pursued jobs in the business end of the medical industry and made as many connections as I could. I worked as a pharmaceutical sales rep for ages until I met enough doctors and heads of hospitals who could help me pull together an investment group where under-funded medical outlets could get what they needed. It's been about three years since I was able to quit my sales job and run the foundation full time." he said.

"I'm impressed, Matt. That's really noble work you're doing. You're like the ultimate charity man. I can't compete." I said, genuinely impressed.

"I really don't see it that way but thanks." he said.

"When my husband died I can't say I noticed any out of date medical equipment. That room was stocked up with top of the line stuff from what I could tell."

What am I saying? I sound like such an idiot.

I didn't have any remarks of worth on medical supplies so I decided to sip my coffee to shut myself up before I said anything else that sounded totally erroneous. I crossed my legs and sat back in my chair. Matt was looking at me very intently all of a sudden.

"Cassie. Was it hard?" he asked.

"Was what hard?" I asked him.

"Andrew dying." he stated.

It was shocking to hear Matt say his name.

"Umm. I'm not sure how to answer that." I said.

I felt a little confused at the bold question but didn't let it show too much.

"I'm sorry if that was abrupt. Of course it was hard. What a stupid thing to ask you. I just know how much it helped to talk about things after my mom died and I felt like I was talking about myself too much. I am so sorry. You don't have to talk about it if you don't want to." he explained apologetically.

"OK. I get that. No, I don't mind talking about it…" I started, coming around to the idea.

This is the sort of thing that Dr. Amdell would definitely approve of. I was supposed to be talking about Andrew's death all the time to help me process it.

"Well, umm. It was hard. Yes. Really hard. Really, really, really hard. It really wasn't in my plans to be alone with two kids and a mortgage at 31. I really didn't think I'd get a call telling me a drunk truck driver came across the freeway at top speed and slammed head-on into my husband's car. I really didn't plan on seeing my husband's body laying there completely mangled and broken. There was so much blood. His face was almost unrecognizable. His legs were smashed. His chest was smashed in. His suit was destroyed. His car was…I had to tell Miles before I told Lydia…"

I swallowed and wondered how long I'd be able to hold my voice together as I spoke. The air felt thick all around me and I paused before inhaling to continue.

"The hardest part was telling the kids. Miles understood what had happened, what a car accident was, but he just couldn't grasp that my husband wasn't coming home ever again. I didn't think Lydia understood at first; she kept asking for him, wanting him to kiss her goodnight at bedtime…he was gone. She cried every night waiting for him to come in and kiss her. He was just completely gone forever just like that. They never got to see him again. They never got to say goodbye…"

I trailed off as I started to tear up. My voice went hoarse as I maintained a low tone. I couldn't speak in a normal volume; my tears were blurring my vision and I knew I'd really start to cry hard if I tried to make my voice sound stronger than it was.

Keep calling him "husband". Don't say his name. I told myself.

"Are you OK?" Matt barely whispered to me.

I nodded not meeting his gaze at first. I inhaled and looked him in the face. He looked shocked, but sympathetic, and full of regret for ever having asked the question. His blue eyes shone in the light of the kitchen as he stared at me.

Our "catch up over coffee" went from zero to 60 really quickly for me. I didn't expect this.

"I can't seem to say his name in front of you. I'm sorry." I decided to admit, still whispering.

"Why not?" he whispered back.

"Because I miss saying it out loud to him. Because then I'll really start crying and it will be unbearable." I barely said as more tears welled up in my eyes.

"It's OK to cry, Cassie." Matt said in a gentle tone.

I nodded.

"I know."

I whispered my response to Matt, knowing that it was OK to cry, but feeling stupid for doing it nonetheless. I had so many emotions packed behind my tears and letting them fall out, in front of Matt, being so vulnerable with him, had me buzzing. I was never this open and vulnerable with anyone else aside from Ruth and Jennifer in the past months.

Matt had made it so easy for me to speak; it caught me off-guard.

"Is there anything I can do to help you through this loss, Cassie?" he asked me gently.

His genuine concern was evident on his face as he stared at me.

"I don't know." I answered honestly, not knowing what else to say.

"I'd like to be a friend to you if you need one." he said.

Matt was so kind, no one had directly expressed what they wanted to be to me in situations like this. So many other times when I got together with other friends or acquaintances, it was clear they just wanted to hear about the drama of Andrew's death firsthand and not actually follow up with any sort of real support.

"I wish I had a friend back in December." I thought out loud, recalling spending Christmas with the kids and not having Andrew there with us.

Matt looked perplexed.

"What do you mean? What happened in December?" he asked.

I felt immediately stupid for saying a word about December. I tried to hold back my new tears as I explained. It took me almost an entire minute to muster the words.

"Christmas was so excruciating." I whispered in a broken voice.

I felt streams of new tears falling down my cheeks and wished I had never even attempted to explain this to him. I glanced up at Matt's face through my tears and felt horrible for the sad and sympathetic expression I had definitely been responsible for putting on his face.

"I'm so sorry. I shouldn't have brought this up at all. I didn't know what else to ask you. I feel horrible." he leaned in a little as he spoke.

"Stop apologizing." I whispered once more.

Matt's eyes were wide and bright. He looked concerned for me. He stared at me for a moment before relaxing his face completely.

"I'll stop, I promise." he whispered.

Matt said nothing as he slid his arm across the table and took my hand in his. His hand was warm and comforting. A pleasant sensation came over me as I let him hold my hand; it was peaceful. I felt my face relax and my body go warmer. He was careful and kind and we sat in silence for a minute. I know he was assessing how closely the blue of his eyes matched the shade of blue of my eyes, because it's exactly what I was doing. I saw nothing else but his bright face and his kind eyes. I only felt the fall and rise of my chest as I breathed. With his other hand, he reached into his pocket and pulled out a piece of fabric.

"Is that a real hanky?" I quietly asked, feeling strong enough to speak again.

"Yes. It was my mother's."

He offered it to me and I took it to dab my cheeks with. As I brought it up to my face I noticed a needlepoint detail on the corner. It was an origami crane outlined with light blue thread.

Chapter 6

MATT

"I should probably go soon." I said carefully to Cassie.

I felt like I had really blown this coffee catch up. My stomach lurched with regret for ever asking her about her dead husband.

"I'm so sorry for turning the waterworks on like this…" she said.

"Now you're the one apologizing too much. It's fine. This is what it's like. Trust me I understand." I said, trying to force a half-smile in her direction.

I felt completely gutted with guilt for asking her such a personal question that caused her to cry. She probably never wanted to see me again after today. What the hell was I thinking?

She smiled back at me, meeting my gaze again with the bluest eyes. They sparkled even more than they had before. She was gorgeous even when she was crying. Her black mascara had run down her left cheek with her tears but she still looked amazing. She didn't have a single hair out of place and her red lipstick was the exact color of her shoes and coat. I had to look away from her more than once while she talked about her husband so that she wouldn't notice me staring at her. It felt like I was gawking at another man's wife. *Stop staring, stop staring, stop staring.*

When I walked up to the diner and heard her scolding a stranger on the sidewalk I knew she was still the same intense and unapologetic person from school. She bowed down to no one; I found it so attractive. She had more confidence than any other woman I'd known. So much gumption. As we walked in the house she shared with Andrew I found myself jealous of a dead man. He had everything a man could possibly dream of. The perfect career and house. Kids. And a wife like Cassie.

I didn't want to, but I released Cassie's small hand like it was the most fragile piece of glass. It almost physically hurt to let go of it. I didn't mean to hold her hand but she seemed so alone and so broken recalling Andrew's accident that I couldn't help myself from taking it into mine. What I really wanted to do was throw myself out of the chair, pick her up, and squeeze her as tightly as I possibly could. I'd tell her to sob for as long as she wanted even if it meant completely destroying my shirt with her mascara beyond all recognition. I restrained myself and settled for the handkerchief instead.

I stood up slowly and carefully lifted my raincoat off of the back of the chair. I pushed it in and watched as Cassie rose from her chair. Not a hair out of place still.

"I like this old school hanky, Matt. I really do." she told me with a true smile.

Her eyes still sparkled with residual tears as she smiled about the handkerchief.

"I carry it with me all the time. I make a lot of women cry." I joked sensing a lighter mood.

"So old school..." she said as she brushed her fingers over the crane on the corner.

I never expected someone to be so enchanted with something so simple.

"You know I always kick it old school, Cassie." I wasn't sure what else to say. *Good one Matt.*

"Do you?" she asked.

The way she looked when she asked me couldn't be described. Her eyebrows were raised slightly, she was smiling, and her eyes looked hopeful.

"Yes." I said.

"Like you use maps and can tie knots and stuff?" she asked.

"Of course. What would be the fun without the challenge of navigation without modern conveniences? I do everything like a real man. Change my own oil, basic plumbing, I can even sew patches. I even know how to bind books." I said.

"You're being serious?" she questioned.

"Of course. I tied knots all the time rock climbing and there isn't a GPS in existence that could take me to some of the places I climbed even if it wanted to." I said.

It was an odd line of questions but I went with it.

"Alright. Cool." she said.

She handed me the handkerchief back, her tears folded inside it.

"Do you want me to wash this?" she asked.

I shook my head with a smile and took it from her, feeling her fingers brush against mine while she did. It felt like small sparks were given to me with the handkerchief. I shoved it in my pocket quickly so she couldn't protest and insist on washing it herself.

"I really liked seeing you and I love your house, Cassie." I said as we walked toward the front door.

The rain had slowed down but it was still dark for being the middle of the day. The woods surrounding her house were damp and dark, but welcoming and full of life. They were as intriguing and complex as Cassie.

We made it to my car without exchanging words. She was never this quiet in high school. I opened the driver door of my car and turned to say goodbye to her. I gathered a few ounces of bravery and inhaled.

"Can I see you again?" I asked, hiding my exhale.

She nodded without hesitation.

"Is there a time next week that works for you?" I asked.

I couldn't rip my eyes off of her as much as I tried. I couldn't get over how beautiful she still was. She somehow looked even better than she did when I knew her. Her life experiences hadn't aged her at all; they made her more visually interesting and more full of life and wit. Her body of emotions was a testament to her personality.

"I might be able to find an evening but I can't sacrifice another Widow Wednesday or my friends will lose it." she said matter-of-factly.

"'*Widow Wednesday*'?" I asked with intense horror.

My heart lurched at the thought of whatever that could possibly be.

"I have to pick up my kids from preschool in a few minutes so I really can't explain what that is right now but they happen on Thursdays so that isn't good for me next week." she said.

"OK…? I'll let you go but can I call you to set something up?" I asked slowly.

I was confused but knew I should get going. I just didn't want to leave without feeling out whether or not she would want to see me again.

"Sure. Call me and we can figure it out." she said.

I almost went to hug her goodbye but stopped myself.

She was so out of my league. I shouldn't let myself get attached to someone who isn't ready for a new relationship. She couldn't even say her husband's name out loud yet. What was I thinking, hoping that there could be anything more than the light high school friendship we once sort of had available to me? Plus, there was so much we still had to talk about. *I need her to know that--*

Before I could continue questioning myself she slid her arms around my waist and nestled her head under my chin in a hug. I exhaled and wrapped my arms around her upper back and held her for a moment. She felt so warm holding onto me; I could have stayed standing there with our bodies pressed together for hours. I breathed in quickly, catching the floral scent of her perfume. It was intoxicating and I had to refrain from doing more than holding her. She felt tiny and vulnerable in my arms. I knew if I didn't break our embrace now that I wouldn't be able to protect my heart from feeling things I knew I couldn't control.

"It was so good to see you!" I said, trying to step back a few inches.

"I really, really like this raincoat." she responded, releasing me.

"OK?" I said back, smiling.

She looked into my eyes as we pulled away from each other entirely.

"Please drive carefully." she said slowly with a serious but friendly tone.

"I will." I said, really meaning it while nodding.

I slipped into the driver seat with a smile and a wave. She smiled and waved back as I pulled away. Before I made it to the end of the driveway something happened to me that hadn't happened in a really long time. I was crying.

The thoughts that had circled my mind for ages all came crashing down together as one large drop from my mind. It felt like an anvil of grief, frustration, and longing was overtaking my body, dropping heavily onto my chest.

I pulled my car over as soon as I knew I wasn't anywhere near Cassie's neighborhood. I flung open the driver door and stood in the dark afternoon on the side of the road next to my car. I bent my knees, locked my hands onto each knee, and stared at the wet road between my feet gasping for air with tears falling out of my eyes sinking into the wet pavement. I felt sick and stumbled to the front of my car, placing my right hand on the wet hood. Once I made it to the other side I vomited into the grass. It became easier to breathe after I threw up and I collected myself after a few minutes of feeling large pellets of rain hit my exposed neck.

I have to tell her next time I see her. I can't live like this.

My stomach twisted at the thought of telling Cassie what needed to be said. I vomited again in the grass twice. Finally,

I felt strong enough to get behind the wheel again. I slapped on my blinker, pulled back onto the road, and headed to my apartment. I drove home in a blur. I was exhausted as I walked inside my front door. I threw down my raincoat in anger when something flew out of a pocket and landed on the floor next to it. It was my mother's handkerchief, still damp from Cassie's tears and streaked with black mascara. Just when I thought I was done throwing up, I found myself running for the bathroom off of the kitchen and hurled into the toilet.

After splashing water on my face, I stripped off my shirt and jeans, both damp with sweat and rain. I slid in between the sheets, put a pillow over my head, and tried to avoid thoughts of Cassie telling her children that they would never see their father again until I fell into deep sleep.

Chapter 7

CASSIE

Lydia snuck into my bed at six in the morning on Saturday. She shimmied her small frame and pressed as tightly into me as she possibly could. Nestling her head under my chin, laying on her side, facing me, I could smell the Spiderman Berry Blast kids shampoo in her hair. She was holding her fluffy pink kitten stuffed animal named Lovely under her left arm and must have ditched her floral pajama pants in the night because I could feel her warm bare legs rub against mine.

"Did you have nice dreams last night, Sweetie?" I asked her in a haze.

"Yes, Mommy. There was a mermaid in it." she replied.

"How wonderful. I wish I was a mermaid." I said.

She rolled away from me and sat up against the pillow on the other side of the bed and pretended to tuck Lovely in for a nap.

I fell back asleep for another 20 minutes dreaming of Andrew. When I woke back up I heard Miles scamper toward the bed. "Mommy!" he rejoiced.

"Come give me a million kisses to wake me up, Miles. I can't wake up." I moaned.

Both kids jumped on top of me and started to smother me with kisses and fake kissing noises. It was pure bliss. There's nothing more adorable than children wearing pajamas first thing in the morning. Plus, it helped that it was too early for them to bicker about anything, complain, or need.

After the children ran out of the room toward the toy shelf, I reached for my phone to find two texts from Ruth and missed calls from my mom and a number I didn't recognize. I wondered if it could be Matt's number. I hadn't heard from him since we met on Thursday and was a little bit surprised.

RUTH

I meant to call you on the way home from work on Thursday. How did it go?

You're probably fast asleep by now, text or call me in the morning with the update.

I hit reply to Ruth's latest text telling her I'd call her later if I had a break.

As I brewed coffee and poured two bowls of cereal for the kids, I caught up with my overly enthusiastic mother about how Thursday with Matt went. All things considered and awkward moments aside, I thought it went pretty well.

I called Ruth next.

"Agent Bond at your service, M." I said as she picked up.

"The joke that never dies I guess." she sighed.

"Oh come on. You used to love Agent Bond's missions." I stated.

"I'm on the edge of my seat to hear how this latest mission went. I've been so curious." she said.

"I wish you'd called me on Thursday night. It actually went pretty well. We never made it to the diner because I guess their kitchen caught on fire like five minutes before we were supposed to meet so I randomly suggested we come here." I told her.

"Here?! As in your house!?"

"I know. Trust me. I was as shocked as you. I didn't mean to offer my house but I didn't think we should try The Back Country. Plus, I didn't even have enough sugar packets in my purse anyway." I said.

"Oh my gosh. I just can't believe he was in your house. Wasn't that so weird?" she asked.

"It was at first. I couldn't even remember my own name when I walked through the front door I was so flustered, but I got it together and we caught up. He does have a cool job like we thought." I said.

"That's great. Did he say anything else interesting? I need to know more."

"Umm… I can't remember now. See this is why you have to call me on the day these things happen. I've done like a thousand things and gone to a million places since Thursday. So many school events in two days. Oh. I definitely cried telling him about Andrew. That was a thing." I remembered.

"Seriously? You were crying?"

"Unfortunately, yes. But you know what? I really wasn't as embarrassed as I thought I'd be. He's comfortable to be around." I said in earnest.

"Wow." Ruth was completely silent. I could hardly detect the sound of her breathing for what felt like over 15 seconds. It was strange.

"You seem a little lost for words, Ruth."

There had never been this much dead air and silence in our conversations in the history of our friendship. She seemed distracted.

"I'm not. I just can't believe it got intense enough for you to be crying, that's all. Did he say anything else?" she asked.

"Not really. Miles! No! Share! I should go, Ruth. The kids just detected that I'm on the phone and I should shower before all hell breaks loose."

My kids always knew when I was on the phone and behaved at their worst when I was.

"No problem! I'll see you Thursday! Pretty great that Jennifer found a sitter, huh?!" she said.

"Yes! I'm so excited to see her! Oh! And bring your hot sauce this time; I've been craving the fajitas and I can't use the natural jalapeno pepper jam they have again. Bye!"

I hung up and began my day.

I successfully put both exhausted kids in a nap at exactly one in the afternoon after going to the park, getting our faces painted at the library book fair, and stopping for milk at the grocery store in town. I could have used a nap myself but on a whim, I decided to call the unknown number in my missed calls.

"Hello?" a man's voice answered.

"Hello. This is Cassie Caldwell. I had a missed call from this number."

"Oh my gosh. Hi! Cassie! It's Matt. I tried calling you last night. I should have left a voicemail." he said apologetically.

"That's OK. I would have never listened to it anyway, those definitely get ignored...just like old emails. I just saw that I had a missed call and I figured I'd make sure it wasn't a client or something." I said.

"How have you been?" he asked warmly.

"Great!" I exclaimed.

"Enjoying your weekend?" he asked.

"Not really." I replied.

"Oh. What do you mean?" he asked, sounding a little shocked.

"I have two kids, Matt. There are no 'weekends.'" I explained.

There was no other way to make him understand since he wasn't a parent so I didn't bother trying to explain further.

"I guess that makes sense." he said, sounding confused.

Classic for someone who didn't have children. They had no clue.

"This conversation feels a little strange, Matt." I declared, knowing it was probably my fault.

"I'm sorry. You're right. I'm super tired today." he snapped to life a little bit.

"Did you call me last night for any particular reason?" I asked.

"Yes. Sorry. I just. I didn't know if you wanted to go to dinner sometime this week. I know you said Thursday's weren't good but I have Wednesday and Friday open if you have the time. I don't want to steal you away from your kids though. No pressure." he said.

"It's so nice to get some words out of you, Matt. I thought I was talking to a stranger for a minute there. That sounds great. I only have Wednesday night open so if that works for you, that works for me." I replied happily.

I knew how awkward this must be for him. He was a trooper for even wanting to see me again at all.

"Awesome. Can I pick you up at your house?" he asked.

"Sure! How fancy are we getting?" I asked.

"Just regular fancy. It's a restaurant-themed restaurant. If I come at six will that give you enough time to be home from work?"

"Six is perfect. Will this 'restaurant-themed restaurant' be on fire when I arrive?" I asked.

"Would you like it to be?" he asked.

"Only if the food sucks." I said.

"I certainly hope that's not the case." he said.

"I'll bring my fire extinguisher just in case. See you on Wednesday."

I hung up while he was saying goodbye so that I wouldn't keep rambling.

I guess I needed to do some laundry so that I'd have "going out to dinner clothes" available by Wednesday. I quietly headed upstairs toward the bathroom where the hamper was. I tiptoed past my kid's rooms where they were hopefully fast asleep. Once I entered the master bedroom, I stopped in front of Andrew's closet.

I have to do this at some point. It's basically been a year. Why are you making this such a big deal?

I dragged the laundry basket to the top of the steps as I delayed walking in Andrew's closet. I just couldn't go in there yet. I decided to start the load of laundry and then go into the closet.

I started the laundry. Then, I meandered into the kitchen and did dishes. I found piles of mail to organize in procrastination. *Just do it. Don't be a baby.*

Finally, I forced myself up the stairs once more and opened the door of the closet. That familiar light cedar smell hit me immediately. I delayed turning on the light and just smelled Andrew for a minute with my eyes closed. I could pretend he was right here with me in the dark. The light would show me reality so I pulled my hand away from the switch. I stood as still as I knew how; if the children woke up and walked in the room now it would force me back to reality more quickly than the lightswitch would. I just wanted to pretend I was with Andrew.

I drifted into a daydream of his hands sliding around my waist. He pulled me closer to his warm face. I could feel him breathing in a measured pattern as his face was right in front of mine. His hands slid under my ears and he pulled my face into his, pressing his lips into mine, and sliding his tongue into my mouth. His hands drifted to the waistband of my jeans, hooking his fingers into the belt loops on either side of my hips. His lips and tongue made their way down the side of my jaw and on to my neck. I was gasping for air, my chest rising and falling quickly. He bent his knees and drug his mouth and tongue down my sternum, slowly approaching the bottom point of my v-neck t-shirt. His hands spread across my ribcage. I could feel my pores opening with sweat. I slammed my eyes open.

I have to stop. I have to stop this.

I ripped myself away from my daydream and Andrew's closet. I gently shut the door and slid against the closed door to sit on the floor. I hunched over bent knees looking at the hardwood floor, catching my breath. This area of the floor was more worn than other parts because this closet got so much use for so many years. I focused on the wear marks on the floor as I breathed slower and slower. I recalled every pair of beautiful shoes he would wear to work and to dinner that crossed over this part of the floor where he walked. He always dressed so well. He never looked like he was trying that hard though.

The washing machine beeped loudly a floor below me, snapping me out of the beginning of a second silly daydream about Andrew's clothes. I stood up, crept down the steps, and moved the wash to the dryer.

Am I really ready for dinner on Wednesday? Am I crazy?

Chapter 8

MATT

I finally had my apartment organized and feeling like a real home but work was an entirely different story. Moving an entire enterprise was exhausting. The last year had been particularly crazy and moving to a new city certainly added to the chaos. The new building was great, the new employees were competent, but I felt completely unfocused. I was so consumed with thoughts of writing to Cassie, seeing Cassie, befriending Cassie… She took over my thoughts and made work feel so boring.

I was lost in the memory of Cassie from the other day at her house when one of the lawyers who worked for the foundation knocked on my door. It was my friend Richardson.

"In ten minutes you're expected to give a statement to the local paper about what your foundation stands for and why you started it, Matt. Make sure you go over all those talking points I mentioned and stick to the script like we talked about." he said.

I stood up from my desk to head down the hall and buttoned my dark blue suit jacket as I rose. I could never dress casually for this job because I was the face of the foundation and often had my picture taken for press releases and interviews.

"Yes, Sir. Be right there." I said as I saluted him while he walked back out of my office.

This should be a blast. I just love talking about my personal grief...

I had started this foundation after becoming disenfranchised with the horribly out of date machines and technology at the hospital where my mom died. We lived in a rural area but it wasn't depressed so there was no reason for the lack of funding. I couldn't imagine how much worse the technology was at places that were actually located in impoverished areas.

After she died, I questioned whether or not my dad and I could have had more time with her if the hospital had been set up differently. I made it my mission to use her death as a motivator to make changes in hospitals all over America for the better and with the hope that other families wouldn't ever have that same wonder I lived with.

My mom was feisty, always sure of herself, but so sweet and so loving. She had a personality that attracted every sort of person to her. Even while fighting cancer, she made her doctors and nurses laugh constantly; she wasn't boring and she always kept people on their toes. If you did something wrong or something wasn't right, she wasted no time making it known. I missed her a lot, but I was happy to have my dark years of grieving her behind me. Meeting Cassie had me remembering her all over again because of her similar personality.

"Matt Brooks, you're all set up I see?"

I saw my good friend, Juan, a doctor from New York who essentially started the foundation with me, standing in the doorway of my office.

"Juan Martinez, yes I am." I replied.

"You forgot to say 'doctor'. *Doctor Juan Martinez*." he said.

"Forgive me, Doctor. I'm not worthy." I joked.

Juan loved to drop his title on people as much as he could. It drove his wife crazy.

"Listen, I know you have a ton of meetings today but I'm finally moved into my place as well and Marie wanted to know if we should have you and what's her name over to dinner?" he asked.

"There's no more 'what's her name'. I cancelled her visit out here." I said, knowing there would be annoying follow up questions and cringing at the thought.

Juan gave me an expressive look of shock and surprise at this new information.

"You seriously aren't dating her anymore? Another one bites the dust. How can this be the case? I see the way women look at you, Matt. You can't stay single forever. What happened with this one?" he said.

"They're all so boring though, Juan. Plus, how do I know if they aren't just into me because of the foundation being so well known? It's hard to trust just anyone." I explained.

I could feel anger at my dating life rising within me.

"That's a good point. Maybe this city will be better though. The people are so much more down to earth and you might not

get recognized as much when you go out since you're new here."
he pointed out.

"Ugh, I don't want to 'go out'... I'm so done with that. I want a
real life, Juan. You have one, what's it like?" I asked.

"What? Real life? A wife? Kids?" Juan asked.

"Yes. Is it great or is it hard, or...?" I asked.

I was pretty sure I knew the answer but I wanted
his confirmation.

"Yes." he said decisively.

"See. I love that. I want that. I don't want some boring dating life with some boring girl who asks me the same questions,
the same small talk, the same restaurants, the same jobs. I want
someone who will really inspire me...Cassie. That's who I want
to be with, Juan. She's incredible. I've never met anyone like her
before..." I said, my voice drifting.

I cringed as I realized that I was rambling.

"Who's Cassie? What am I missing?" Juan asked with
raised eyebrows.

"She's a girl I went to high school with who just so happens to live a half hour from here. I have a major crush." I
admitted sheepishly.

I began to close all the tabs on my computer screen while
I talked with Juan.

"If you went to high school with her wouldn't she have
a husband and kids by now? You could be a little late my
friend."

Juan looked at me with a knowing expression.

"She has two kids. Her husband was killed almost a year
ago." I said, clearing my throat.

"You're going after a *widow*?!" Juan said way too loudly.

My eyes widened at his loud statement.

"Shh! I wouldn't call it 'going after'. I would never do that. I can't imagine she'd be ready to move on yet. Do you know how hard that would be? All I know is that I have a crush on her and she's still as amazing as I always remembered. I don't know if I'll ever get another chance with her so I feel like I have to take it now; I'm just trying to be friends with her. I'm not trying to take advantage or anything. That would be so wrong." I said, disgusted at the thought of anyone trying to take advantage of Cassie's current status.

"Now?" Juan asked.

He had clearly only picked up on the 'taking a chance now' part of what I had explained. He looked amazed.

"Yes. Literally now. I'm taking her to dinner."

I was logging out of my computer and looking toward the door to leave for home to change before heading to the suburbs.

"Not yet you're not. You have to make that statement and that new lawyer is here so you'll be stuck in the meeting for at least an hour." Juan said.

"Are you serious? That meeting is now?" I asked, frowning.

"We could play hooky and go to the gym instead." he offered.

"I'll definitely go with you later this week but I shouldn't miss this meeting. If you want, call me tomorrow and we can see if Richardson wants to get lunch with us sometime as well."

I was in full business mode now that I knew I'd have to rush to make it in time to take Cassie to dinner. It couldn't come soon enough.

Chapter 9

MATT

"I'm wearing a suit like an idiot." I said as I walked around to the other side of the car to open the passenger side door for Cassie.

"You're wearing a suit like an idiot?" she asked with a puzzled expression.

"Yes. I thought I'd have time to change after work but every meeting I had today went late. I'm so overdressed." I said in slight frustration.

"What really defines 'idiot' though? And who even makes the rules with clothes...maybe the real idiot in this situation is me because I'm not wearing a suit? Who really knows what's normal anymore?" she asked in a joking tone with a big smile.

"Are you going existential on me?" I asked, smiling back. "I'm definitely the one who doesn't look normal."

"I just have a lot of gumption. Take me to dinner, Driver." she replied, her smile beaming.

Cassie looked incredible, of course. She was wearing dark skinny jeans with really, really, shiny pointed black leather flats with giant bows near the toe of each one. Her black pea coat was perfectly pressed and buttoned halfway up. Her hair was perfect as always, with long blonde waves, and her blue eyes were light with happiness. She wasn't downcast at all like the last time I saw her at her house.

I felt confident as I drove down her driveway again, temporarily forgetting that I had to rush to get here. My last meeting at work was excruciating and time flew by so quickly. I realized at about 4:45 that I was stuck in this dark blue suit for dinner. I felt frazzled as I sped out of the office toward Cassie's suburban town. Now, behind the wheel with Cassie next to me, I relaxed.

We caught up on work and she told me more about her kids as we headed to dinner. I took a breath as I reached to open the passenger door.

"I hope you're hungry, Agent Bond...Caldwell." I said with a smile.

What the hell am I saying?

"Smooth." she laughed.

"I have no idea what I'm saying. All I can picture is your email address written above your head when I see you. You make me want to watch all the James Bond movies." I said.

I had a flash of a daydream of watching movies with Cassie for an entire Saturday on my couch.

"I tend to have that effect on people and honestly it was a cooler last name then Caldwell." she explained.

"You don't like Cassie Caldwell?" I asked.

"No, I love it. It just doesn't have that secret agent vibe. It sounds like someone who designs purses. 'Oh is your purse a "Cassie Caldwell"?!' middle-aged women would be asking each other on the sidewalk of Talbots and Anne Taylor. The purses would cost $79.99 for no reason at all. All purse prices are completely arbitrary. Everyone knows they're all made in China."

I laughed at her impression, relieved to hear her sense of humor again. We sat down at the table and discussed the menu. Cassie wasted no time remarking on what looked great and what seemed horrible.

"Who in their right mind would ever order something as horrific as snails?" Cassie declared in a horrified whisper across the table.

"I just can't get my head around this concept and I don't want to try." she said.

At first I thought she was joking, but seeing her serious expression reassured me she wasn't. I was thrilled to know she hated something I also hated.

"I agree 100%. I've tried to like delicacies like that for years and I just can't get past it. I'm just fine eating steak or chicken like a regular person." I said.

Cassie smiled at my honest response and narrowed her eyes on me the slightest bit.

"I have an important question for you Matt, and I don't want you to be offended." she lowered her menu.

"You can ask me anything." I said, beginning to worry.

Cassie leaned in over the table to get closer to me and lowered her voice. I forced myself not to get lost in her eyes as they caught the flicker of the candle between us.

"What are your drink expectations right now?" she asked.

"What do you mean?" I asked.

"Like what are you expecting to drink? With your dinner." she asked.

"Umm...I hadn't given it much thought. I'm driving so probably water." I answered.

Cassie looked nervous.

"OK."

"OK? Is that OK?"

I was desperate to know.

"Yes."

We looked at each other for a few more seconds in silence. I tried to work out what she was thinking.

"I'm sorry...that I just asked you that, Matt, but I had to know what your plan was." she finally exhaled.

"It's fine. It's not a big deal." I said.

My brain finally clicked inside my head and I completely understood why she was verifying my plan so I wished that she wouldn't keep explaining it.

"Surely, you can see why I'd want to know. I have a strict 'I only ever have a drink at home' policy for myself and I didn't want to push that on you but I had to know what you were thinking." she said, seeming a little shy.

"Don't call me 'Surely'." I joked, feeling desperate to change the subject.

What an idiot. What a stupid joke; everyone's sick of that joke.

"Seriously, it's fine Cassie. I wouldn't dream of drinking and then getting behind the wheel like--"

I stopped myself. This conversation was heading into dangerous territory. *Why do I do this?* With perfect timing, the server approached the table. I was so relieved for the distraction and complete change of subject. *Thank God.*

Cassie chatted almost endlessly throughout our dinner. We had plenty to relate to regarding our jobs. She worked in public relations for years and made mention that it was only boring "about 35% of the time." I was grateful for her talkative nature because I could hardly eat my steak medallions and hoped she wouldn't notice and think less of me. I couldn't imagine that Cassie, as opinionated as she was, would consider someone to be a real man if they couldn't eat like one.

Her face lit up as she told me about her family, friends, and work. Her personality was as attractive as her face and body were. I continued to ignore my dinner and found myself lost in her animated face. Dinner was almost over and I had to know if I could see her again.

She was going on and on about a tree in her yard that was struck by lightning. I had no idea how the conversation landed there but the way she described the thunderstorm and flash of light was completely engrossing. I handed the waiter my card without glancing at the check because this story she was telling was like a vortex I couldn't not be sucked into.

"Will you show me the tree?" I blurted out.

"The tree? The lightning tree? You want to see it?" she asked with slight surprise.

"Yes. The lightning tree. It sounds insane!" I said with a little too much enthusiasm.

"Sure! I'd love to show you the lightning tree." she said, absolutely glowing.

"When can I see it?" I asked.

I had never taken such interest in a damaged part of nature in my entire life.

"Well, it will be too dark by the time we get back, but you can come on Friday evening if you want. I'll have my kids at home but if you don't care, I doubt they would. They love showing people that tree."

She seemed thrilled.

"I'll be there."

I had to see that tree. I had to see Cassie. I had to talk to her more.

On the drive back to Cassie's house, I drifted deep into thought while she chatted. It was so easy to just *be* with her. She was confident yet vulnerable, caring yet feisty. I began to worry that what I thought was just a residual crush from high school wasn't as simple as that. I was really taken with Cassie, much more than I thought I would be after seeing her only one time before tonight. I imagined us driving for hours together and adored the thought. Before I could respond in detail to anything she was talking about, we were pulling into her driveway and I felt my nerves all over again. My stomach flipped.

With clammy hands, I shut the car off and walked behind the car to open the passenger door. Cassie was already standing up outside of the car when I came around to the other side.

"I was getting that for you." I said.

"I can do it myself." she declared with a smile.

I was standing just inches away from her and felt my nerves even more.

"I know you can, but that's not the point." I smiled. "I kick it old school, remember?"

"True. How could I have forgotten? I'm just usually hustling out of my car as quickly as possible to get my kids out and into school or wherever. I'm never the passenger anymore. I don't know how to be one it seems." she said.

I stood back a few inches so that I wouldn't lean forward and kiss her perfect lips. It took everything in me not to.

"You're allowed to just ride along sometimes." I said.

"You're right. I should learn how to do that sometime. Sage advice, Mr. Brooks." she said.

A peaceful look came over her face as her smile faded just a little bit.

"Thank you. Thank you for dinner." she said.

I walked Cassie to her front door. It was pitch black dark outside even though it was 9:30 at night. Her front flagstone path was lit by the two large copper lanterns on either side of her front door. She held her light blue purse up to the right side light to find her key. Suddenly I had no idea what to do with my hands. I pulled them in and out of my suit pants pockets, I adjusted my jacket with them, I tried holding them at my sides. Nothing felt natural and I wished I wasn't so unhinged. I felt nothing like myself.

Cassie found her keys, unlocked the door, and looked at me to say goodbye.

"Thanks again for dinner. I'll see you Friday for the tree?" she asked.

"Absolutely!" I laughed nervously.

Chill out.

Cassie stepped forward with a smile to give me a hug so I opened my arms wide and took her into my chest. I inhaled her incredible scent and tried to remember how to stand normally on two feet. I felt her small frame within my arms and felt my heart lurch inside my chest. I quietly exhaled to try to calm myself, found her cheek with my lips, and kissed her cordially.

My throat tightened and my heart pounded against my chest as I considered saying something. I couldn't bring myself to open my mouth to release words so I kissed her cheek once more, muttered a goodbye, turned, and walked back down the flagstone path to my car.

"Hey Matt!" I heard Cassie shout from behind me a full ten seconds later.

I turned around. She was still standing on the front porch. She looked striking as she stood under the lantern of the porch; it was like a spotlight on her entire body. I nervously walked back toward her with a look of confusion and hidden delight on my face.

"What's up?" I asked as I looked right at her.

She inhaled calmly before she spoke.

"Was this a date?" she asked.

She was leaning against the front door. She looked relaxed for such a bold question. Her face was completely neutral so there was absolutely no way for me to know how she wanted me to answer. I wracked my brain for the best response. It had felt like a date in every single way, but I never meant it to be a date when I initially asked her to dinner. I wanted to be her friend. I had been through personal tragedy myself recently and I figured I could be a friend to her in ways others who didn't know what it felt like could be.

I ran my fingers through my hair with both hands before I opened my mouth to speak; my heartbeat had not slowed down in the least bit. I stepped onto the third step, about three feet away from her, forcing myself to keep a real distance. I looked at her in the eyes, her face looked expectant. I didn't dare not answer her.

"Sorry to peg you with such an odd question, but you seem nervous so I thought I'd ask…" she explained before I could speak.

This woman had somehow read me like a book. I didn't even feel surprised; she probably knew exactly what my heart rate was by looking at my face.

"Cassie… I didn't mean it to be when I asked you to dinner, but I guess it sort of was…" I said.

I prayed that I had answered the way she wanted me to. Her face remained neutral as she took in my answer. She pondered it for 30 seconds before speaking.

"OK." she said confidently.

"Is that OK?" I asked with the slightest desperation.

"I think it is. I think it was a date." she said, her face looked sure.

"So, are you saying that we're dating?" I asked.

I knew it was a risk but I felt like I had to know and it was clear that we weren't afraid to ask each other bold questions. I felt desperate for solid answers when it came to Cassie.

"I think I am saying that. It's weird for me though…you should know that." she said, her face slightly less sure than before, but still confident.

"I don't want you to feel like you're rushing anything…" I said quickly.

"I think I should. I think I should try dating someone. You. Specifically. I think it's good. It's good for me if it's good for you." she said as her thoughts unfolded in her head.

I was surprised in the best way and couldn't hide my delight as I stepped even closer to her. I held my hands out to her and forced myself not to say anything stupid that would blow this new development. Knowing she felt this way was overwhelming. Knowing she was willing to take a shot on dating me after her husband died felt like an honor I didn't deserve.

 She hesitantly took both of her hands and placed them in mine. I smiled at her and felt warmth spread from my hands to my arms and hit me in the chest like a bullet. She offered me an unsure smile through the trace amount of fear she was wearing on her face. I rubbed the other side of her hands with my thumbs in an attempt to alleviate her nerves which were now adorably on display.

"It's good for me. We don't have to rush anything. Whatever you want is fine with me, Cassie." I said quietly.

She nodded. I released her hands even though I could have lingered with her for longer. I knew this was a big step for her and I didn't want to scare her away. I said goodnight again and walked back down the path to my car. I finally exhaled, but my heart was still beating at lightning speed. I pulled out of the driveway smiling like an idiot. I didn't expect Cassie to admit to want to date me. It felt impossible.

I turned out of the driveway and onto her road when my thoughts changed. Once again, I felt nauseous. I forced myself to at least make it a few miles past the last place, on the side of a random country road, where I'd vomited after I left Cassie's house before I pulled over.

Calm down. Just breathe.

I opened the door and stood slowly out of the car in the cool, dark air. There were no other cars around. I fumbled to the other side of my car and heaved into the grass. *This is ridiculous.* I felt anger rising inside me.

I only threw up once. As I slid back into the driver seat, I detected the scent of Cassie's perfume lingering in the car. It smelled clean, sexy, and downright blissful. Spending time with Cassie was really messing with more than just my head. The effect she had on me while she wasn't even still sitting next to me felt unreal. I angrily pulled my arms out of my suit jacket and tossed it in the backseat along with my tie, then slugged back gulps of water from a water bottle in the pocket of my car door to reset myself.

I was exhausted and enraged with myself as I walked into my empty apartment. I promised myself I'd stop throwing up all over the roads of western Pennsylvania. I ripped off my shirt, unbuttoned my pants, and sat on the edge of my bed with my head in my hands. *This is like living inside a nightmare and a sweet dream. Why can't it just be one instead of both? I have to tell Cassie next time I see her. This is just getting pathetic.*

I reached inside my pants pockets to take out my keys and wallet to put them on my nightstand when my fingers found my mother's handkerchief. I had put it inside my pocket before I left to pick up Cassie in case she needed it again. Thank goodness she didn't or I'd still be throwing up on the side of the road.

I woke up to a new email from Cassie. Before work even started, we found ourselves emailing for hours.

6:29am
FROM: agentcasbond@hotmail.com
TO: matt.brooks@tmbf.com
SUBJECT: The Lightning Tree. Very Important.

Dear Matt,

Thank you for dinner and thank you for being so honest with me. I hope I didn't freak you out. I'm super rusty when it comes to anything involving dating.

Mostly, I'm emailing you because I wanted to make sure you were fully prepared to see The Lightning Tree. I bet it will be the highlight of your new life here in Pittsburgh. Are you excited, Mr. Brooks?!

Agent Bond

I smiled and responded.

6:38am

FROM: matt.brooks@tmbf.com

TO: agentcasbond@hotmail.com

SUBJECT: Attire for The Lightning Tree. Also Very Important.

Dear Cassie,

I've waited my entire life to see this famous Lightning Tree. I'm thrilled beyond all belief. Should I wear anything special to see it? A tux?

Will wait for your reply…

Matt

7:00am

FROM: agentcasbond@hotmail.com

TO: matt.brooks@tmbf.com

SUBJECT: There's nothing more important than attire.

Dear Matt,

If you personally own a tuxedo, you'll have gained many, many points, and will have earned almost every ounce of respect I have. I reserve my respect for people in most situations, but you might be able to level up a few if you actually own a tux. How sophisticated of you, Sir.

Color me impressed. But to answer your question: no tuxes required for The Lightning Tree. I'd recommend Normal Person Themed Clothes.

Agent Bond

7:13am

FROM: matt.brooks@tmbf.com

TO: agentcasbond@hotmail.com

SUBJECT: A valid point. Clothing is serious business.

Dear Cassie,

I'm ready to receive any and all accolades you have to give because I do, in fact, own a tux. I also want you to be prepared to have your mind blown because, not only do I own one tux, but I own TWO!!! For visualization purposes: one is black and the other is navy blue, my best color, at least in my opinion.

I'm so excited to have advanced so quickly on your respect scale. Seems like it would be a hard one to stand on.

I hope your day is going well, can't wait to see you and The Tree on Friday.

Love, Matt

7:36am

FROM: agentcasbond@hotmail.com

TO: matt.brooks@tmbf.com

SUBJECT: !!!!!!!!!

MATT!!!

You aren't serious!?!? TWO OF THEM!!?? I'm shocked and awed beyond all belief. Picture or it didn't happen. I'll be waiting for those all day. You have my number.

My day is stupid. I'm hating myself a little bit for replaying old (and wonderful) conversations from years and years ago. Have you ever wished you could go back in time? If I could, I wouldn't have said so many nice things to my husband. It would have made things in my marriage crappy instead of great and then maybe I wouldn't feel as sad.

Is my logic twisted? Am I insane? Is this that early 20's angst we discussed?

Share any and all thoughts.

Agent Bond

7:50am

FROM: matt.brooks@tmbf.com

TO: agentcasbond@hotmail.com

SUBJECT: I'm glad you like that I have tuxes.

Dear Cassie,

I regularly wish I could go back in time, but I don't know that I would have said MORE crappy things to people. I know the feeling of longing you're experiencing and to be honest, it's making me feel a little less ridiculous for sending you those emails years ago. Thank you for being just crazy enough to expose that side of yourself to me. I needed to know I wasn't alone with my email ramblings. To answer your questions though: you aren't insane and your logic isn't twisted. The past is a weird place to dwell. Don't beat yourself up for anything.

Please don't be sad today. Your smile is so bright and it's already been raining all day.

Love, Matt

8:02am

FROM: agentcasbond@hotmail.com

TO: matt.brooks@tmbf.com

SUBJECT: Prepare yourself for a personal
question

Matt,

You say the nicest things. What's a guy
like you doing still single?...seriously. Now's
the part where you tell me about your last
serious relationship.

I'll go first: I was married for like eight
and a half years and then my husband died. The
End.

What've you got?

Agent Bond

P.S. It's technically been raining all week.*

8:30am

FROM: matt.brooks@tmbf.com

TO: agentcasbond@hotmail.com

SUBJECT: Should I think of a personal question for you now?

Dear Cassie,

Oh how fun! I was really hoping we would get
to this part of the show!

OK, I'll be man enough to tell you about my
past lovelife. I guess I'm a grown up and this

is what grown-ups who date do???

I've had three serious-ish girlfriends in the past 10 years but I never felt like anyone measured up to "Matt-standards". What you need to know about "Matt-standards" is that even I don't know what they are. I've just followed my gut and have known for a fact, A BIG FACT, that none of those women were ever going to be the one I'd want to settle down with.

My first serious girlfriend from college wasn't anything like me and I knew it would never last.

My second serious girlfriend chose a job over me, which is ironic, because I also chose a job over her.

My third serious girlfriend was very nice. Very, very nice. Almost too nice. She was so nice that I started to question if it was real, I found reasons to pick the entire relationship apart and decided that it was real and that's what bothered me. Who tips a valet who dented their car? Who enjoys everything they eat at a restaurant? Who invites people who have stolen money from them over for dinner? She did. That's who. I came to the conclusion that her personality was non-existent and this was a problem. She lacked fire.

I broke up with her about six months ago and I was casually seeing someone until about two months ago. I got gold-digger vibes from her so

I guess you can add that, and being too nice, to the red flags for "Matt-standards." Again, I'm still figuring it out.

On the subject of standards, I can't even begin to imagine what "Cassie-standards" would be. You are one of a kind and I don't say that lightly. Also, eight and a half years is almost a decade; color me impressed.

Love, Matt

P.S. Does it ever stop raining in Pittsburgh?

8:40am

FROM: agentcasbond@hotmail.com

TO: matt.brooks@tmbf.com

SUBJECT: I dare you to try.

Dear Matt,

Wow. I asked you about your LAST serious relationship, not your entire dating history. Points will be deducted for not playing the game correctly. And thanks, eight and a half years was impressive. I'm patting myself on the back right now.

As far as Cassie-standards, I think I'm re-defining them as I go along. A lot has changed since I had to think about what they were so I'm not sure of my own framework beyond, don't murder me, have a job, love children, don't do drugs, and don't dress like a slob...

I think what has remained from my high
school and college years would be: Don't Be
Boring. Way to go, Mr. Brooks; so far, so good.

Agent Bond

P.S. It will stop raining just in time for
the snow to start.

P.P.S. Pittsburgh is still better than New
York though.

8:48am

FROM: matt.brooks@tmbf.com

TO: agentcasbond@hotmail.com

SUBJECT: Do you sing in the shower?

Dear Cassie,

I'm going to do my best to live up to your
standards. I won't be too boring if you promise me not to be too nice. I should probably
actually stand up from my desk at home and go
to work now. Thank you so much for the hours of
distraction. I'm checking my phone and I officially have 12 missed calls. It's totally worth
it.

I can't wait to see you on Friday, Cassie.
Have a better day.

Love, Matt

P.S. I guess at least if it snows, I can eat
it. Have you ever eaten snow before? It's my
favorite flavor. Is that weird?

P.P.S. Of course Pittsburgh is still better than New York; no arguments from me on that one.

9:02am
FROM: agentcasbond@hotmail.com
TO: matt.brooks@tmbf.com
SUBJECT: Of course I sing in the shower.

Dear Matt,

My day is so much better than it was going to be because of your emails. You beat me: I only have four missed calls. Looks like someone's day is about to be way more busy than mine. Hint: it's you. That sucks. Good luck getting through this one my friend…

See you on Friday, still waiting for those tux pictures…

Agent Bond

P.S. Eating snow is weird, but I do eat snow. Literally all the time. I love it.

Chapter 10

CASSIE

It was Thursday morning: Widow Wednesday. I had spent hours avoiding work and emailing Matt instead. I had to rush to get ready to leave for The Back Country Diner. I considered being cranky at the thought of having to answer tons of questions about seeing Matt again from Ruth but then I immersed my thoughts into the emails Matt and I had been sending each other all morning.

Plus, I remembered that this time Jennifer would be there and she would offer news about her life so maybe that would take some of the heat off of me and my latest endeavours. It became quite wearing, being the one everyone asked questions to all the time.

I didn't know what to think of myself at this current moment. If I was being honest with myself, I clearly wasn't over Andrew with the strong possibility of actually never being over him. On the other side of things: it felt great to go out to dinner with Matt. It was incredible to go out to dinner without children and act like a real grown-up again. I selfishly enjoyed how attracted Matt obviously was to me and definitely couldn't deny how attracted I was to him. No one could deny how handsome he was in his suit; every woman in the restaurant last night had to rip their eyes off of him while passing by our table.

I was glad I asked him if we were dating. I needed to know and it needed to be understood where I was. I was conflicted but I knew that Dr. Amdell would think this was good for me. I knew it was good for me. I needed to take a small step to move on, even if it felt confusing and a little scary.

I brushed off my thoughts and feelings of confusion, guilt, longing, and excitement while I got myself pulled together to meet the girls at The Back Country. I rushed to make it on time so that I might get a few minutes alone with Jennifer before Ruth came. I was too late and saw them both waiting for me at our regular table. Jennifer stood up to hug me.

"It's been wayyyy too long, Cass!" she exclaimed.

"I've missed you so much and I'm dying to see this baby!" I said.

I leaned down to see her six month old daughter Lucy sitting in her car seat with a pacifier. She was adorable and looked twice the size she was the last time I'd seen her.

"Give me that baby!" I said, getting her out of her car seat.

"I'm here too!" Ruth said on the other side of the table, already setting sugar packets out.

"Oh hello there, M!" I said back to her.

"Cassie, Ruth tells me you're seeing someone?!" Jennifer

chimed in as I bounced Lucy.

"Are you freaking kidding me, Ruth?" I glared toward her.

"What?! Aren't you?!" she looked genuinely surprised I'd question her.

"Ruth. I'm HARDLY dating him. It's just a guy from high school reconnecting with me, nothing more." I said.

"'Reconnecting', is that what they call it these days?" Jennifer asked.

"You've seen him twice now…" Ruth said.

"It's really nothing. It's not a big deal."

I felt a cranky feeling coming back. This wasn't how the conversation was supposed to go. I didn't want to be questioned on this and the fact that Ruth had already talked to Jennifer about it didn't sit well with me.

"I think it's great if you're just seeing him as friends, Cass." Jennifer said, trying to reel the conversation back to neutral.

"Thanks, seriously that's all it is. We went to high school together. He's just a guy…we are going really slowly…" I said, trying to do the same.

"Sometimes 'just a guy', can turn into an actual boyfriend, Cassie." Ruth stated out of the clear blue sky.

"Wow, you got there quickly, Ruth. No one here said anything about a 'boyfriend'…"

I had to be visibly angry by this point because Ruth picked up her menu and began to study it intently even though we never look at the menu at The Back Country because we only ever ordered the same four things. I decided to change the subject before things really went south.

"Jennifer, I want to know everything about this baby and about Danny and about your life."

Jennifer caught us up in a lengthy fashion. I was thrilled for her slow pace of updates but still burned about Ruth's suggestion that Matt was my boyfriend. She was never the same about relationships since she and Jared broke up right after I had Miles. She would go on and on about how everyone else was moving on with their lives and growing up but she was moving backward being single again. As much as Jennifer and I consoled her, it never quite took all the way.

Her comment had to be coming from a residual feeling of jealousy. I went all the way: got married, had kids, a house, and white picket fence and even after my husband died, finding someone new wasn't difficult. I tried to ease up on my anger toward Ruth once I realized that not everyone else had it so easy in the romance department. It would be short-sighted of me to think that this wouldn't be hard for her in a completely different way than it was for me.

I carefully studied Ruth while Jennifer talked about Lucy's eating schedule. She looked distracted by her phone, her lipstick, anything within reach. She stirred her iced tea with her straw endlessly, making a harsh ice crushing sound each time she shoved the straw back into the glass. Once she stopped that she moved to constantly fidgeting with the small mountain of sugar packets in the center of the table. She'd stack them in three rows of four, four rows of three, and so on. Next she ran outside to "take a client call" in the middle of Jennifer's story about her husband's promotion. Finally, Ruth returned to the table in a fluster.

"Sorry girls. I had to take that call. Work has been insane." she said out of breath.

"That's too bad." I said flatly.

"Don't even worry about it. You didn't miss anything." Jennifer said calmly.

"I should actually get going. I have a meeting in an hour I really have to prepare for. I hate to rush off like this but this is a really important client and he'll probably be waiting for me in my office when I get back from lunch." Ruth said.

"Don't worry about it, get going. Will I see you next week?" I asked as we all stood to hug Ruth goodbye.

"Of course!" she said with too much enthusiasm.

Jennifer and I waved as Ruth rushed out to the parking lot. Jennifer used the opportunity to run to the bathroom without her baby while I sat at the table with Lucy still on my lap.

I looked at Lucy in the eyes and she looked right back at me with a neutral face.

"Well Ruth was pretty freaking weird today. What was that all about?" I asked Lucy.

She looked at me blankly with drool sliding down her chin.

I bid Jennifer farewell and made her promise to come see us more. She promised as she loaded Lucy into her car. Hugging her goodbye made me long for the simpler days in college. We always had such a blast. She would forever be a large part of the night that Andrew and I met and I've never taken that lightly. She could have been a total brat to him and chased him off that night but she stayed calm and trusted a stranger with her friend. I loved her for it.

I headed to my car and brushed off my thoughts of Ruth. She wasn't herself but it wasn't up to me to figure out why. *She's probably just jealous.*

I felt snooty even thinking it, but it could have been the case. She just didn't have as much success in her relationships. I told myself to let it go as I pulled into my driveway.

After tucking my kids in that night I noted the calendar. I had 13 days until the anniversary of Andrew's death. It was really, really time to make some real progress on the closet.

Don't be a baby, actually do this. They're just things.

I pulled a black tank top over my head, slid on my pajama shorts and a thread-bare cardigan from college and opened Andrew's closet door without hesitation. I took a deep breath and grabbed a bin of socks first. I set the bin against the wall opposite the closet. *See. That wasn't so bad. Go for the pants.*

I did just that. All the jeans and work pants were folded and stacked against the wall with no issue. Next I reached for Andrew's suits. They were really nice. As I held up the dark blue one, I thought about Matt before I could even stop myself. I thought about the look on his face while he held my hands on the front porch after we decided that we were dating. He looked incredible in that suit. The thought came so naturally to me, but so abruptly, that I audibly gasped and jumped back from the suit section of the closet.

What was that?

I declared myself done for the evening and gave myself a time out by walking downstairs and sticking my head in the refrigerator. *Doctor Amdell would call this 'tangible progress'. Pat yourself on the back and stop freaking out. Our thoughts do not define us.*

With my face pressed up against the top shelf of juice boxes, carrot sticks, and individual containers of guacamole, I forced myself not to cry.

Pull yourself together and buck up, Cassie. Stop being a baby. Stop making everything such a big deal. It didn't mean anything. Our thoughts do not define us. You're allowed to move on.

I stepped away from the fridge, grabbed some large bags from the pantry, and began heading toward the stairs to pack up Andrew's clothes that didn't remind me of someone I had seen twice recently who was "just a guy". I refused to let Ruth's words from lunch echo in my brain as I stuffed the socks and pants into the bag.

Matt wasn't Andrew. Andrew wasn't Matt. These men were in two different categories. I had nothing to worry about and I was pretty sure my therapist would call this evening "progressive progress". *I'll take it…*

It was definitely time for bed. Tomorrow held another day of shuttling children, work, and the anticipation of weird feelings related to Matt coming over on Friday. I heard my phone ding from inside my back pocket and reached for it. Matt had dutifully texted me two pictures.

One was of him wearing his black tux at what looked like a very formal wedding. He clutched the side of a newly married couple with a huge smile on his face, looking the most attractive I'd ever seen him. The second picture was of his navy blue tux. My eyes widened and I audibly gasped when I glanced at it, almost having to turn my head away. He somehow looked even more handsome and was holding a microphone, clearly the MC of a benefit or event. His smile jumped out of the picture. His skin glowed under the lights and he looked like a movie star. I fanned my face off with my hand and scrolled down to what he wrote before responding.

MATT

So I definitely shouldn't wear either of these to see that tree tomorrow???

CASSIE

Matt. I feel a slight obligation to tell you that you were right. Navy blue is definitely your color.

MATT

 I imagine it would be yours as well...

Since we look like siblings!

CASSIE

I think I might regret pointing that out now. I am imagining what we would look like posed for a family picture in the 90's both wearing navy blue. People would assume we were fraternal twins.

MATT

Stop saying such sexy things.

CASSIE

We'd both be in braces.

MATT

With a teal fabric backdrop?

CASSIE

Of course.

MATT

If we were siblings, we wouldn't have these names. We'd be named Randy and Sandy or something equally awful.

CASSIE

Torrie and Lorrie.

MATT

Which one is Torrie and which one is Lorrie?

CASSIE

No one knows.

MATT

I can't imagine it anymore...it's too creepy. I prefer that you aren't my sibling thank you very much.

CASSIE

The feeling is mutual.

MATT

Glad to hear it.

CASSIE

Glad to feel it! Have a good night.

MATT

Sleep well Cassie.

Chapter 11

MATT

"So how'd it go with the widow?" Juan asked with a smile. He asked the question innocently, but had no idea how awful it sounded to me.

"'The widow'? Never say that again, Juan." I snapped.

I was having a hard time sipping my coffee. I rubbed my eyes with exhaustion. It was the end of what felt like a really long week. It was difficult to keep my breakfast down this morning even though it was a single egg and piece of toast. I was still reeling from seeing Cassie. Our conversation about drinking at dinner had me a little terrified. I would never drink a drop again if that's what she would ask of me. Our email exchange felt incredible though. I felt like she was so open with me and it was easy to be open with her. I felt butterflies in my stomach when I thought about going to see her tonight. I couldn't believe how casual she was about letting me meet her kids; I didn't expect it but I was thrilled. *This is way too many feelings…*

With perfect timing, all three of the foundation lawyers stepped into my office with notebooks and laptops ready for our meeting. They chatted loudly among each other, adding to my frazzled state of mind. I looked at them with a frown.

"We don't have to have this meeting in my office you guys. You know there's a perfectly good conference room right down the hall…" I explained while pointing in the direction of the conference room.

They noisily marched out of my office gathering their things back up and taking them down the hall.

"Juan, let's make this meeting happen so that we can get it over with." I said, ushering him out of my office and feeling a sudden desperation to accomplish something worthwhile.

"I'm ready, Boss." he said.

"Are we on for lunch with Richardson later?" I asked him as we walked toward the conference room.

"Yes. He said he was good to go. I'm sorry about before, Matt." Juan said, looking apologetic.

I shrugged it off. He didn't know what he was saying.

"I had no idea you cared so much about this girl. How did your dinner go?" he asked with genuine interest.

"Fine. Good. Really well. Too well…" I said as I recalled how easily Cassie and I were able to talk and how hard it was to leave her house as I held both of her hands in mine.

I felt warm all over just thinking about it and caught myself beginning to smile at the memory of the way her hands felt in mine.

"So what's gonna happen with her?" Juan asked.

"No clue." I said, snapping back to reality.

During the meeting, I drifted back into thoughts about Cassie and felt bad butterflies in my stomach when I remembered what I was keeping from her. I forced myself not to think and just made my mind go blank for the remainder of the meeting. The meeting with the lawyers went well enough but I was relieved to leave the conference room where I was beginning to feel like a prisoner of my emotions and of the battle in my head to think and then not think. Richardson, Juan, and I headed downtown and sat at our table for lunch.

"This city isn't so bad." Richardson said as we glanced at the menu.

His eyebrows rose in delight as he read down the page and scratched his dark brown beard. It was as wild as his curly dark brown hair. Richardson looked nothing like a traditional lawyer. He belonged at sea. Or on top of a mountain.

"I told you guys that Pittsburgh was the right move. The hospitals around here are so much easier to work with and it's more centrally located in the U.S. It's calmer here, less expensive..." I said.

I could think of a thousand more reasons why Pittsburgh was the better option but I didn't need to because Juan and Richardson already knew. Juan rolled his eyes.

"Yeah, we know. You've explained this to us hundreds of times. Are you sure this move doesn't have to do with your dad dying?" he asked.

"Plus, we know that you'd do anything to leave New York. I also hated it there, by the way." Richardson chimed in.

"It has nothing to do with my dad." I assured Juan.

"Well, whatever the case, we are loving it here and I think we can call this a successful transition." Richardson said.

I agreed and wanted to eat my lunch to celebrate with them but barely could. Richardson noticed my lack of appetite.

"Matt, you're rail-thin and you've barely touched your lunch. What's the matter with you?" he asked.

"Nothing. Work's just crazy. I'm fine." I replied quickly.

I understood why one meal would cause him to ask this. I had thinned out way more than I wanted to over the past months. Even my slim fit suits felt slightly loose. The last thing I wanted to discuss was my lack of appetite and how I'd vomited all over the side of the road on the way home from seeing Cassie. Who I was dating. This felt like dangerous territory with Richardson so I changed the subject quickly and forced myself to eat every bite of my sandwich. Once I did finish, I was glad I did.

Chapter 12

CASSIE

Friday's drive home from work was standard. A light drizzle of cool rain fell out of the sky as I loaded Miles and Lydia into their booster seats. They loaded into the back of the car with their little backpacks and colorful coats zipped up to their chins. I kissed both of them on their rosy cheeks after I buckled them in.

We pulled onto our road as I explained to them that a friend of ours was going to come see the tree that was struck by lightning over the summer and that if they wanted to tell him all about it, they could. Miles was too busy telling me about a new game at school to care much and Lydia wasn't even listening. She was counting the raindrops that splashed onto the window as we drove.

"1,2,3,4,5,8,9,10,20, twenty one hundred, forty..."

The kids played perfectly while I changed out of my work

137

clothes. Because the temperature had taken a small nosedive today, I pulled on my jeans and white T-shirt, and figured a sweater would make sense. I searched in vain for a heavy cardigan all over the bedroom until I noticed the bags of socks and pants across from Andrew's closet. He had tons of really nice sweaters. *I should just grab one of his, they're all so warm. This isn't a big deal. You took all those other clothes out with no problem.*

I held up an olive green wool cardigan with large brown buttons. I touched the buttons carefully as I felt the combination of soft and rough fabric under each finger. As I held it closer, it finished unfolding itself. Suddenly, the scent of Andrew's cologne, permanently trapped in the fabric, released itself and crashed into me with a flood of memories. *Oh gosh. Please not now. Please, please, please.* I pleaded with myself not to cry, not to break down, not now.

It was too late. I lost all the air in my lungs and my vision went blurry with tears and dizziness. I squeezed the sweater close to my heart and heard myself gasping for air. It felt like Andrew had just died in my arms. He was gone; he was gone forever. I remembered that I wasn't just taking a vacation from my real life right now. It wasn't some weird dream; Andrew was never coming back. I struggled and gasped for air as I fell to my knees and wept on the floor of the closet. I clutched the sweater with soaking wet hands. My face, arms, legs, all soaked in sweat. I tried to quiet my now audible sobs by pressing the back of my wrist into my mouth. If the children saw me like this, they would be even more scarred for life. I wiped the tears, snot, and drool off of my face with the back of my hand.

My head pounded as my sobs slowed and I slowly caught

my breath. Still squeezing the sweater tightly in my arms, I tried to sit up a little. It made my pounding head and aching heart feel even worse. I laid down on my right side to try to regulate my breathing as I lost track of time. I opened my eyes and saw Miles standing over me.

"Mommy, what are you doing?" Miles asked.

"Oh nothing. What are you doing, Honey?" I asked back as normally as I could.

"Playing with Sissy. Why are you in here?" he asked, his blue eyes wide with curiosity.

"Oh no reason. I just wanted to lie down where it was nice and cool in the house. Mommy got so hot just now." I responded.

I tried to sound like this was something I did all the time. *Be normal, be normal, be normal.* Before Miles could question me again, we both heard a ring at the doorbell. *Shoot. Matt's here.*

I heard Miles and Lydia run as quickly as their little legs could take them down the stairs and to the front door. They loved visitors. I figured the kids would stall Matt with their chatter for a minute so I decided to roll on my back to try to actually cool down, open up my chest, and get a few exhales out before I stood up too quickly and really made this worse. I would look like a mess if I ran downstairs right now, plus, I still wasn't breathing normally. *The way these kids chat, I have at least 90 seconds before I have to be back to normal. He'll probably love meeting them.*

It was too late. The next thing I saw was Matt standing over me while I laid on my back on the floor of the closet. He was wearing jeans and his wonderful, proper, navy blue raincoat unzipped with a T-shirt underneath. He dressed perfectly casual and looked just as handsome as he had in his suit. His stature was impeccable from this angle.

This is great. This is just great. Way to go, Cassie. You're even crazier than those Other Diner people.

"No tux?" I asked in a casual manner as though it were completely normal to be laying on the floor of a closet with a tear-stained, sweaty face, holding a man's sweater when a guest arrived.

"Cassie, are you OK? Were you working out just now?" Matt asked with a concerned look of confusion on his face.

"'Working out'? Don't be ridiculous, Matt. I'm having a panic attack." I said nonchalantly as I lay there motionless, not knowing what else to do.

There was no reason to lie. Plus, if this guy wanted to actually date me, he should know how ugly things could get sooner rather than later. This would give him a chance to run for the hills if he felt inclined.

"Oh my gosh, are you serious?" he asked, clearly horrified.

"Don't worry. I'm completely fine." I mumbled.

I slowly sat up as Matt bent down onto his knees to get closer to me.

"I don't need any help. Don't worry." I said, waving him off.

Matt looked completely shocked.

"Cassie..." he said, almost as a question.

"I'm fine. Seriously." I said quickly, trying to quickly assess the state of my hair with my hands.

I had to reassure him that this wasn't a big deal, but mostly I wanted this closet interaction to end before my kids came upstairs. I communicated this with my face, looking toward the hall and stairs. He took the hint and stood back. I assumed he would leave the closet entirely but when I didn't hear footsteps leaving, I looked up and saw him standing over me with his hands extended to me.

I reluctantly took a hold of both of his hands and let him pull me up to standing. I opened my mouth to thank him but before I could get my words out, Matt had pulled me into a tight hug. With my head pressed against his warm chest, I felt myself recover from gasping for air.

"You don't have to explain anything to me, Cassie. I completely get it." he said quietly above my head.

I felt my heartache both increase and decrease at the same time as I caught my breath. He said and did all the right things but it was happening in all the wrong places and times. We were standing in Andrew's closet with his green sweater on the floor in a heap below us. My kids were somewhere in the house and could appear at any moment. Matt's hug and words were so comforting; I felt an odd peace about this completely random interaction as Matt held me. I never got this kind of encouragement and my panic attacks were always my own to overcome and deal with in the past year.

"Thank you." I whispered to Matt, still in his arms, feeling his heart beating against me.

He was right, I didn't have to explain myself. We broke apart and walked out of the closet. Matt kept a hold of my left hand and gave it a kind squeeze.

"Did you really think I'd work out wearing jeans in a closet?" I asked, attempting to lighten the mood.

"You don't work out in confined spaces with heavy fabric?" he joked back.

His smile was warm and his handsome face was glowing with life.

"I don't always work out in confined spaces with heavy fabric, but when I do, it's right before someone is coming over." I responded with a smile.

"Your kids answered the door and said you were upstairs. I'm pretty sure your son thought you had a sprained ankle because he said, 'Mommy's leg is hurt upstairs and she can't walk.'" Matt explained, his face amused.

"What a liar. I definitely never indicated that to him." I said, rolling my eyes.

"Your kids are both in your basement now, by the way. They said something about getting their lightning rods from down there. I think they were getting me one too." he said.

I considered how far away the basement was from the master bedroom where Matt and I stood. It was such an intimate room, yet Matt was completely natural standing with me inside it.

"Oh yeah, they think that lightning rods will protect them from the lightning powers from the tree. We better get one for each of us." I said smiling.

"Let's do it." Matt said.

Matt released my hand and watched as I walked over to the sweater, picked it up, and folded it before setting it on top of the bag of socks and pants against the wall. We walked downstairs as I called for the kids. They each came running upstairs with stacks of sticks in their arms.

"We only need one lightning rod for each of us, Miles. Put these other ones back in the basket. Lydia, go get your shoes if you want to go to the tree." I ordered.

A few moments later, the drizzling rain had stopped and the four of us were walking outside toward the grouping of trees about 100 yards behind the house. We each held a stick. Miles and Lydia were talkative and natural around Matt which was an odd relief. I let Matt walk up ahead with the kids while I enjoyed a break from everyone a few feet behind.

Matt looked genuinely enthralled with the children as he engaged them in conversation, pointed out types of leaves that had fallen off of the tall trees above, and picked up cool sticks. He looked even more gorgeous outside in the evening light. His blonde hair almost glowed in the sunset lighting and his eyes were bright with life as he laughed with the children. He looked so tall next to Miles and Lydia. I adored watching my kids, but I couldn't take my eyes off of Matt. He was so wildly handsome and even though I'd noticed his good looks before, they were jumping out at me in a way they never had until now.

"So who is this?" he asked Lydia, pointing to her stuffed pink cat.

"It's Lovely." she quietly replied.

"She is lovely. But what's her name?" he asked kindly.

"Lovely. Her name is Lovely. She's a baby kitten. She doesn't eat real cat food though." Lydia explained.

"Oh! Her name is Lovely. That's the perfect name for her! Did you name her that or did your mom help you?" Matt asked.

"Daddy did." Lydia responded.

She reached for Matt's hand to hold. He held it carefully and let her lead him toward the lightning tree which was now just ten feet away. It was beautiful to witness and I effortlessly shrugged off any blend of guilt that my mind tried to feel.

I was jealous of the children's carefree nature with Matt though. They didn't overthink anything. They didn't have to. I couldn't even get a sweater out for this evening without having a breakdown. I decided that I wouldn't allow my thoughts to poison my mind; I wanted to enjoy this evening and appreciate the break from our normal Friday nights of popcorn and a movie. The rain had stopped and there was someone new to share a piece of our lives with. I had so much to appreciate.

I caught up with everyone else as we came upon The Tree. It had once been a huge Oak that stood probably almost 100 feet tall. It was now black and dying, a quarter of it's height, charred, and ugly with no leaves on it. The huge gash in the center of the tree was the most interesting part to see.

Miles imagined that a small bear would live in it now because it looked a lot like a small cave had been carved by lightning in the center of the now short tree. The kids recalled the loud boom and bright light in detail for Matt. He listened intently as they described the sounds and sights. I corrected a few points of the story but ultimately let them tell it. They started with the facts of the thunderstorm and ended by telling Matt the reason we each needed the lightning rods before running off to find more. They climbed all around the tree; Miles smacked his stick against it while Lydia tried to tuck Lovely into bed against it with some fallen leaves.

"Evidently, if we don't have these sticks while we're here, the lightning powers will make us blind. We have to have these for protection from the residual lightning left in the tree or we'll be cursed for thousands of years." Matt repeated to me.

Miles had also wasted no time regaling Matt with made

up stories about the various animals and bad guys that the tree had killed with its powers.

"Yes, sir. We take the lightning powers of this tree very seriously." I explained with a serious expression.

"I can see why you would. Look at this tree, it's crazy..." he said in wonder.

He was enjoying this tree way too much. He had clearly lived in the city for way too long.

"It's disappointing to me that the tree isn't still hot from the lightning. It's powers would seem more real to me if it was as hot as the sun or something..." I explained.

While the kids ran over to the other end of the backyard to collect more lightning sticks for their basket, Matt stepped closer to me with concern in his eyes. The brightness of his face had dimmed.

"Cassie listen I want to talk to you about--"

"Matt. Don't. I don't think we need to. Seriously." I shook my head, not wanting to recall my recent embarrassment.

"No, I'm not talking about just now. I want to talk about--"

"Can whatever it is wait? I'm super annoyed at myself for ever even going in that closet and I feel really badly you had to see me like that. Please let it go." I begged him.

I wanted to have a good Friday night and it had gotten off to such a weird start. That last thing I wanted to do was unpack my panic attack with Matt.

Before he could respond, both kids came running with huge smiles and armfuls of sticks.

"Wow! You have a million lightning rods!" I exclaimed.

"Mommy! Mommy! We have so many!" Lydia yelled with delight.

We took the piles of sticks inside and counted them. After Lydia decided she had 5,000, (13), and Miles counted that he had 25, (21), they ran downstairs to put them in the lightning rod basket in it's designated spot in the basement (next to the fireplace).

As we followed them to the basement and sat on the couch in the living area, around the corner from where shelves of toys were, the kids went on and on to Matt about having more adventures in the woods. Naturally, this led to one of my least favorite topics: rock climbing.

"Anyone who's ever gone rock climbing or climbed a rock of any size, will tell you about it within minutes of meeting them." I said, rolling my eyes.

Miles was awestruck at the idea of scaling the side of a mountain. I shooed him away so that he wouldn't get any funny ideas about rock climbing in his future. Matt laughed as we recalled his old emails.

"I'm so embarrassed, but I don't regret climbing those rocks one bit. Those were some of my best times in college. The workout is incredible." Matt said smiling.

"I just can't take anyone who rock climbs seriously. It's a death wish and I don't see the point." I said.

"No way! It was pure bliss, completely exhilarating. Therapy for the mind, body, and soul."

"I'm going to pretend you didn't just say that." I rolled my eyes dramatically.

"I'm serious! You should try it. It will change your life. I still go sometimes, you know..." Matt said with a bold smile.

His passion brightened up the entire basement.

"I'll think I'll stay right here on dry land. I can hardly walk up stairs without tripping; imagine if I missed a hook or didn't strap my harness." I said, shuddering at the thought.

"I can't imagine that you'd be that clumsy. You're always so put together."

"I really am super clumsy. I trip in heels all the time and have more than once slid down the steps on ice. Once, after breaking up with my old boyfriend Jack, I was so clumsy that I ran right into a telephone pole and got a concussion. I had a giant bruise on my forehead for weeks." I explained.

I recalled the night I met Andrew without bringing that part up. It didn't apply to the conversation and I was having a good time with Matt. *More progressive progress.* I looked at Matt's face again as I pondered my small win internally and noticed a strange expression on his face.

"Did you say, 'Jack'?" Matt asked slowly.

"Yes. Jack Richardson. He was an avid rock climber so I think that's where my aversion to the concept began. You'd probably love that guy. He would go on and on about climbing rocks all weekend. I just remember wanting to tell Jack to get a life and talk about literally anything else." I continued, as I ran through some old memories of Jack in my head to myself.

He was a fun guy and I had an overall good association with my thoughts of him. I looked at Matt. He looked as though he had just seen a ghost. I opened my mouth to question him on his odd expression but he beat me to it.

"You were Jack Richardson's girlfriend in college. Jack Richardson from Michigan." he stated, looking slightly nervous.

"Yes. Wait. Did you just say 'Jack from Michigan?' Do you know him?" I asked with wonder.

"Umm...yes...he was one of my close friends in college out in Colorado. We did a lot of rock climbing." Matt said, looking rather pale and uncomfortable as he spoke.

I began to pick up on the fact that there was something he wasn't saying.

"Matt, did you know it was me who he was dating while you were friends?" I asked as my heart began to race a little bit.

"Yes." Matt answered with a guilty look on his face.

"Wait. So you knew about me in college? You knew who I was dating? You were friends with one of my college boyfriends?" I asked.

I was confused.

"Yes." he said with a small nod.

"So you were one of Jack's super awesome friends I heard about constantly and actually talked to on speaker phone a few times?" I questioned as I connected one dot.

"Yes." he said again.

I felt so puzzled. How could Matt not have said anything? He sent all those emails and here I was dating his friend and he didn't say anything about it.

"What the hell, Matt?" I asked.

I didn't know what else to say. Matt and I just stared at each other blankly for a moment. Thoughts of a time in my life when I was completely carefree blended with the present moment. Somehow I remembered a clue from one of his old emails.

"I should have known. You mentioned seeing me pumping gas while you were coming from John Roberts' party in one of your emails. That's where I met Jack. How did I not see you at that party? Why wouldn't you have said something in another email to me, or to me in person, or over the phone all those times? You could have reached out at any time Matt..." I stammered.

I was lost for words and didn't know how I was supposed to feel. Matt swallowed and inhaled.

"Cassie. It's not that simple." he uttered, looking a little resigned.

"What can that possibly mean? You knew your close friend from states away was dating someone you knew in high school. Worlds collided; why wouldn't you have said anything?" I asked intensely.

Matt looked partially guilty and partially desperate. The color in his face came back as he became more and more intense as he spoke.

"It wasn't just one of those small world things, Cassie. It should have been me that night. It should have been me who walked up to you and re-introduced myself, but Jack beat me to it. Every guy in our group of friends wanted to go over to you and shake your hand. Every single guy in the entire party wanted to walk over to you and have a shot. I regretted bringing Jack to my hometown as soon as I saw the way he looked at you when we walked through the door. I shouldn't have let myself fade into the background because that's not who I am...until I'm around you...I should have walked over to you and opened my mouth to say something but I was too scared. I just emailed you instead, hoping you'd never read it, never knowing that I had blown a chance on seeing you again." he explained.

Matt ran his hands through his hair in frustration before he continued.

"High school, that night, all the years after: I should have just called you or found a way to see you. I just wasn't brave enough. I should have told you I was there and that my crush on you hadn't gone away. I know it's crazy but there was just something about you. There still is. You intimidated everyone around you, Cassie: you were so much greater than whatever was happening around you. Who you are as a person literally transcends everything around you; I've never seen anything like it. And I like it! It was so fascinating to see someone who always had it so together..."

He was nearly standing up now and I could tell he was getting hot. I felt a little flustered by his passion because I really didn't see it coming in this sudden monologue. His body language was a major tell that his attraction to me hadn't wavered in the past 15 years. No wonder I could practically hear his heartbeat on the night I told him I wanted to date him.

He looked in the direction of where Lydia and Miles were playing on the other side of the finished basement. Even the cooler temperature down in the basement wasn't stopping either of us from feeling warm with tension. I know that my heart was racing so his had to have been.

"This could have all been mine. But I didn't have the guts to walk over to you back then and I didn't have the guts to tell you even after you and Jack started going out. I didn't even tell Jack that I had known you. He was so smitten and I didn't want to ruin that. I've forever been 'the good guy', always finishing last." he said.

He paused and inhaled before continuing. I listened with intention and wonder.

"The worst part is that I had a chance after he told me you

broke up with him. I still didn't do anything. I couldn't bring myself to say anything to Jack or to you. By the time I had the guts and felt like I was good enough for you, Jack mentioned you were engaged. And here we are…years later…and I'm back to feeling like a complete idiot around you."

Matt's years of self-doubt lingered in the air between us along with my recent disbelief. Thoughts swirled in my head at a rapid pace.

"So is that how you knew that I had kids when you mentioned them in your letter? Is Jack how you found out about Andrew dying?" I asked plainly.

"Sort of." he said, still looking uneasy.

I didn't push him for more words or explanation; he had spilled enough of his guts tonight in my basement and I knew when to stop pressing a man when it comes to protecting their emotions. I still wanted him to understand one thing.

"Matt. If I've ever given you the impression that I've had it all together then you aren't very observant. I might be intimidating and confident, but I don't have it all under control. You've forgotten very quickly that it was less than three hours ago that you found me in a heap, on the floor of a closet, because I smelled my husband's cologne on a sweater. I'm not pulled together by any sense of the word." I explained.

It was my turn to become flustered while spilling my guts.

"Do you know how many times I've gone in that closet and tried to take even one thing out? It's taken me almost an entire year to make any moves. I have been a mess this entire past year. I've hidden my tears behind sunglasses in the grocery store. I've cried to the point of not being able to speak in front of my children. For an entire week, I couldn't even walk on one entire side of the living room because I saw our wedding pictures on the far wall. I won't even go down the road about trying to parent alone. I'm constantly questioning what's OK and what's not. I've questioned seeing you over and over in my head. I don't have my head on straight all of the time. I'm not greater than what's happening around me, Matt. I'm just here surviving...sort of."

Matt blinked at me. We had both made huge confessions and knew how monumental this could be. In my mind, I could almost see into the future and see Matt there. There was no way something coincidental on this many levels could amount to nothing.

"Matt. I don't think you're a creep or anything if that's what you're worried about." I reassured him as I reached for his hand.

I really meant it. I wasn't mad at him in the slightest bit. He hadn't done anything to lose my trust; he was honest with me about his feelings and communicated them as well as anyone would in the situation. He took my other hand in his and moved closer to me on the couch. Both our hands were sweating like teenagers who were in a basement with no parents home. I felt like I was back in high school with the high school version of Matt I was just getting to know.

"Are you secretly in love with me or something?" I half joked, trying to lighten the mood.

Matt looked at me with an expression I could not read.

"I had a high school crush and never acted on it. I blew my shot every time and I feel stupid for not telling you. I really like spending time with you and you've let me into your life without hesitation after you've been through so much. I didn't want to blow it again." he confessed, quieting his voice as he looked into my eyes.

I didn't know what to say because he didn't actually answer my question which made his intentions feel a little vague. I just looked at his handsome face instead of speaking.

"I'm really sorry if this was a lot for you, Cassie. I didn't mean to freak you out." he said sounding a little resigned.

"It's fine. I'm glad to know how you felt." I said.

I still didn't know what to say.

"You don't deserve any bombs like this. I feel horrible." he confessed.

"Listen. Matt. I really like spending time with you. Just be honest with me and don't feel like you have to hold anything back. And please, please, please stop apologizing." I said.

I didn't question what was going on. I didn't need to wonder what he was thinking. Now that he had confessed that he had essentially never gotten over his high school crush on me, things felt more out in the open. I felt as though it changed the dynamic between us for the better. I liked having transparency with whatever was going on between us. I couldn't deny my attraction to Matt and he, more or less, told me that he couldn't deny his attraction to me. I decided against talking about it anymore. I was a willing participant in whatever this dynamic was and was glad that nothing felt out of place or unnatural with him. I felt relieved.

"Please just don't ask me to go rock climbing with you." I said with a warm smile.

"I promise." he said, looking visibly relieved.

The mood was officially lightened. Matt's thumbs brushed over my knuckles, back and forth, sparking more physical chemistry between us. I swallowed.

"Do you actually mean that?" I asked.

I detected a smile creeping onto his face.

"Do I actually mean I 'promise not to take you rock climbing'? You don't want to come with me and feel completely exhilarated?" he asked, his face expressive with the first giant smile I'd seen on him in minutes.

He looked relaxed and confident, it was the best he'd looked yet. It seemed like now that he had taken so much off of his chest, he was filled with pure happiness. He was as handsome as he looked in the tux pictures.

"Yes." I whispered.

Oddly, I felt like I could hardly speak all of a sudden. I couldn't take my eyes off of Matt's gorgeous face. He glanced toward the direction of the kids who were around the corner in the play house, completely out of sight. His face fell out of a smile to a solemn gaze when he looked back in my direction. I knew what was on his mind and I felt my own anticipation inside me. I was excited and nervous as he looked at me right in my eyes and slowly brushed my hair to either side of my face. My heart raced as he edged closer to me on the couch. I couldn't hear anything as the blood rushed to my head. Matt turned slightly to my right as he leaned in toward me even more. I felt him breathing closer and closer to me.

"Cassie." he whispered to me, just inches from my face.

"Yes?" I somehow spoke back to him in barely a whisper.

"You are so beautiful." he whispered in my right ear.

I could only breathe; I felt incapable of uttering a response. My heart was absolutely pounding behind my shirt.

"Can I kiss you?" he asked quietly, his voice even quieter than it was a split second before.

I licked my lips. The butterflies in my stomach felt as

though they would lift me off of the couch and into the air. Matt's hands were on either side of my face, making me feel so warm, so adored.

"Yes."

I breathed out the word.

Matt's lips were warm and soft as he pressed them onto mine. I leaned in even further toward him, setting my hands on his knees. I silently gasped as his lips moved slowly against my lips and as his tongue met mine. It had been so long since I kissed anyone, I'd nearly forgotten how. I forced myself not to count the months inside my head as I opened my mouth more and tipped my chin to my right. His face was warm and smooth against mine. I moved my hands up to his shoulders as we continued, shivers ran down my spine the entire time. He opened his mouth even wider, pushing mine further open with his. He practically sucked me in with his mouth, even stronger than before, sucking and gently biting my lower lip; I could feel him smile against me.

His arms felt so strong and warm as I ran my hands down them. I hadn't touched the defined muscles in a man's arms, or a man's skin, in what felt like forever. I processed each individual muscle, every groove, every hard edge, until I found his strong shoulders again. His neck felt like it was glowing with warmth beneath my fingers as my hands slid all around it before they landed towards his face. I felt awestruck touching his neck. It connected to his face so flawlessly, the way the muscles of it moved as his mouth moved with mine, the rise of his Adam's Apple, everything about it was so incredible to me somehow.

We kissed for another short moment as we both remained very aware of Miles and Lydia right around the corner. We broke apart hurriedly, hoping not to get caught. I wiped my mouth with the back of my hand before he leaned into me again, pressing his forehead against mine, and trying to catch his breath through his smile. His eyes staring into mine; his hands on either side of my face, affectionately cradling it.

"Cassie..." he whispered, his chest rising and falling close to mine.

I was just as out of breath as he seemed to be, but it was time to get the children to bed and I knew that if I didn't stand up now, I wouldn't be able to stop myself from kissing Matt again. I imagined the kids' looks of shock and used it as motivation to rip myself away from him. I signaled in Miles and Lydia's general direction with my eyes as I stood up. I felt completely weak in the knees and had to use Matt's shoulder to steady myself from wobbling.

"I have to put the kids to bed." I said quietly with a sheepish look on my flushed face.

I swallowed and thought about how to begin toward the side of the basement where the children were. As I tried to turn around and walk away, Matt swiftly pulled me close to him once more.

He reached for my waist from behind with both of his strong, warm arms sliding around it. He brought his mouth close to my ear and whispered. I felt his warmth overtake my entire body and a shiver go down my spine as he spoke.

"I promise I won't make you go rock climbing, but I'll warn you, that's a little bit what it feels like." he whispered.

I couldn't imagine that rock climbing would be as exhilarating for me as the past two minutes had been.

Chapter 13

MATT

I lay awake in bed almost an entire hour before my alarm went off on Saturday morning. I had driven home from Cassie's house in a blur last night with thoughts of our kiss at the forefront of my mind; I had replayed it over and over. *I can't believe I got to kiss her.*

I was still in slight disbelief and felt like I was floating. She looked so gorgeous standing in the woods, the sunset lighting on her glowing face as she watched her beautiful children run around the fallen leaves. It looked like a picture and I wished I'd had my camera to capture the moment for her. Her children were personable in a way I didn't expect from kids so young. Cassie was clearly an incredible mother. I had wondered what Andrew was like as I watched his kids playing and laughing. I wondered what he looked like, what his voice sounded like, and how he acted around Cassie. Was he as smitten with her as I was even after being married for years? He had to have been. Cassie would never have chosen someone who wasn't completely crazy, over the top, in love with her. Whoever married her would have had to have been one of the best people who ever existed. A small wave of sadness washed over me as I thought about her husband.

Normally I'd rush into the shower after getting out of bed, but I had so much time this morning. I wandered into the living room and sat on the couch, grabbing a mug of coffee on my way. Pulling an old yearbook out from the shelved coffee table, I flipped to Cassie's picture. She looked almost exactly the same now, as she did then. Long blonde hair and a wide, mischievous smile on her lips jumped out of the small black and white photo. Her smile now was less mischievous; it had more of a genuine quality to it. I flipped to the back of the yearbook to see if she had signed it that year; I couldn't remember if she had written anything. I found her message, written in bright blue ink on the back cover of the yearbook.

Matt! Have an amazing summer— thanks for helping me ace geometry and thanks for never being as boring as that class was!

Agent Cassie Bond

I smiled at the message and her handwriting. I thought about how much more vulnerable and open her life experiences had made her now compared to high school. I wondered if I had matured in the same way. Cassie had somehow matured but maintained the same fire she always had.

The way I found Cassie when I stepped into her house had been heartbreaking. I wondered if she had panic attacks regularly. What if she wasn't ready to move on? She had opened herself up to me but her husband's sweater was so triggering for her. I understood. There were things that I struggled with regarding my parents deaths. It sometimes made normal experiences more difficult than they needed to be.

I turned my thoughts back to the more exciting and happy parts of last night and again, remained lost in thought about kissing Cassie. Her lips were smooth and her hands were gentle touching my entire neck. I could perfectly imagine the feeling of her fingers on my Adam's Apple and how they moved to the back of my neck. The hairs stood up on the back of my neck just recalling her touch there. The way she felt my arms was like she was trying to remember something. Last night I could have kept kissing her, kept stroking her face, and running my fingers through her long waves of hair. I was so lost in thought that I almost spilled the coffee in my hand when I heard my alarm beeping from the bedroom.

I began my day on such a positive note. Aside from kissing Cassie last night, I had successfully unloaded past information on her and wasn't rejected when I told her how strongly I felt. I was meeting up with Juan and Richardson this morning but decided that I wasn't going to them about last night. It felt too soon and I didn't want to jinx myself.

I decided to send her an email before I headed out the door.

7:15am

FROM: matt.brooks@tmbf.com

TO: agentcasbond@hotmail.com
SUBJECT: Rock Climbing later?

Dear Agent Bond,

I hope your weekend goes well even though I know it doesn't really count as one. Miles and Lydia might be weekend ruiners, but I truly enjoyed meeting them. Thank you for that. You're an amazing mother, anyone who meets your kids will know that.

Cassie, I seriously can't wait to see you again. Can I kiss you again? You can say no if you want, just holding your hand would be enough.

I am going rock climbing later; are you sure you don't want to come?

Love, Matt

I received an email back from Cassie just minutes before walking out of the door to drive to the woods to meet up with Juan and Richardson. I smiled at my imagination of her, sitting at her computer, also holding a cup of coffee, in pajamas as she typed pieces of her heart to me from half an hour away.

7:25am
FROM: agentcasbond@hotmail.com
TO: matt.brooks@tmbf.com
SUBJECT: Hard pass.

Dear Matt,

Thank you for your kind words. It felt good to read that someone thinks I'm a good mom. It isn't easy but it's great. Miles and Lydia keep talking about you so they aren't the only ones who left wonderful impressions last night. Also, two things:

Yes. No need to stick to just hand holding.

No. I will never go rock climbing with you.

You'll have to keep your rocks to yourself, Mr. Brooks. I could die up there and then who'll raise my kids?

Agent Bond

I blinked as I re-read the email. *Was that filled with contradicting double entendres or am I still waking up?* I set my keys and phone down and pulled up the chair closer to the desk to respond.

7:32am

FROM: matt.brooks@tmbf.com

TO: agentcasbond@hotmail.com

SUBJECT: I forgive you.

Dear Agent Bond,

Wow. I don't even know how to respond to that one. Either way, I'll be hanging from the side of a cliff in the middle of the woods today but I'll try to call you later if you'd like.

Love, Matt

P.S. Why don't we just call each other now in-stead of emailing or even texting?

She replied before I could get back out of my chair.

7:39am

FROM: agentcasbond@hotmail.com

TO: matt.brooks@tmbf.com

SUBJECT: I wasn't apologizing.

Dear Matt,

Whoops! My game isn't what it was in high school, college, or even a few years ago. I'm completely out of practice. You have me all atwitter, Mr. Brooks. I have completely forgotten what human touch with another adult felt like. Plus, when I woke up this morning, I remembered that I have a date with the graveyard soon and I'm not thinking quite straight.

Agent Bond

P.S. This is more fun. It makes me feel like I'm in high school again; it's a welcome break from real life. A friend once said to me that "Adulthood isn't as much fun as I knew it wouldn't be."

I responded.

7:48am

FROM: matt.brooks@tmbf.com

TO: agentcasbond@hotmail.com

SUBJECT: Very strong-willed about the rock climbing aren't you?

Dear Agent Bond,

I'm sorry about your upcoming date with the graveyard. I know what that feels like and it isn't easy. If you want me to hold your hand, (seriously, just hold your hand, as a friend), I can. But I know it's something you'll probably have to do on your own.

Love, Matt

P.S. I take those words back now. Adulthood just got a lot more fun for me.

8:00am

FROM: agentcasbond@hotmail.com

TO: matt.brooks@tmbf.com

SUBJECT: About that and everything.

Dear Matt,

I'll definitely be going alone, but I appreciate the offer. I'll confide in you that I'm nervous for this specific date. This particular guy probably won't talk back to me which will suck,

(you know how much I hate silence!). Plus, I really don't want to cry anymore this year. It's
just been so hard and I want to get to the other
side of it...

You're allowed to hold my hand anywhere else
in the world, Mr. Brooks.

Agent Bond

8:08am
FROM: matt.brooks@tmbf.com
TO: agentcasbond@hotmail.com
SUBJECT: I like that about you.

Dearest Cassie,

It would be my honor. Also, don't be nervous
for your date. Those particular dates require a
specific kind of bravery I am confident you'll be
able to muster. You seem like a pretty fearless
person. You aren't just one or the other though.
You're pretty and fearless.

Be brave. Thank you for confiding in me. I'd
adore holding your hand anywhere else in the
world.

Love, Matt

Finally, I ripped myself away from the computer with my
heart pounding.

Chapter 14

CASSIE

Another almost two weeks had passed since I'd seen Ruth or Jennifer. Jennifer had actual excuses for not being able to meet up with us on Widow Wednesdays, but Ruth's excuses were thin. I was particularly annoyed with her when she didn't even pick up my phone call the night before the anniversary of Andrew's death. I became hot with tension and anger when I heard her voicemail message instead of her actual voice.

"You've reached the voicemail of Ruth Hodgekins at Trask, Sepler and Roe Law Firm. Please leave a message and I'll return your call as soon as I can. Thanks and have a great day!"

Awesome. This is fun.

I felt more annoyed the next day on the anniversary of Andrew's death than I was sad. His parents insisted on releasing balloons and I didn't think it would be something Andrew would have wanted. It was the exact thing that he and I would have made fun of but, it served as a very present reminder that sometimes your family are the people who know you the least. My in-laws insisted it would be good for the kids so I didn't argue. I knew they were grieving this day as much as I was and wanted them to have a say in what happened. I left the balloon release at the graveyard feeling agitated and tired. My plan was to drop my kids off at preschool after the balloons and head back to the graveyard alone.

After dropping off Miles and Lydia, I couldn't go back as quickly as I wanted because my phone never stopped ringing with condolence calls from friends and family. My mother held me up for an entire hour while I watched random groups of people come and go, in and out of the graveyard. They were all getting their moments and mine was being delayed by so many other things. I wanted to get this over with and my nervous energy was making me jittery. Rehashing this day this much was making it feel so much like the actual day. I was filled with nerves.

Finally, I was able to get out of the car after being parked for ages waiting to return to the headstone. I carefully picked up the paper crane I had folded the night before while I was on the phone with Jennifer reminiscing about the night she and I had met Andrew. She admitted to thinking he was so handsome when she first saw him in our hallway. I smiled as I recalled not being able to properly see his face for minutes until he sat down next to me. We chatted about my wedding, our couples trips, and his personality in general. He was so consistent. Jennifer and I both wished we were more even-keeled the way Andrew was. It was such a great personality trait that really balanced me.

I folded five paper cranes until I made the perfect one I deemed worthy of his headstone. He would have been proud of my precision; it took him weeks to teach Miles, Lydia, and I to fold these cranes and he was ecstatic when it was obvious I had finally nailed it. I tenderly set it in my purse in preparation for this next day.

I was a basket of emotions as I approached his grave. It was a clear day and oddly warm for November. I didn't think of anything but Andrew as I sat in front of the headstone. I sat down with my legs crossed beneath me. My coat spread all around me and my hair hanging at my side felt like blinders. The ground felt cool under me. I began to cry as I thought of his body beneath me, under six feet of this cold ground. I morbidly tried to work out how it would compare to what it looked like a year ago. He felt so far away from me.

Unexpectedly, I started thinking about what it looked like when he was actually beneath me when he was alive. I recalled what it felt like to be with him in bed and how much I missed it. My pattern of thoughts would have seemed strange to others but this wasn't unusual for this past entire year. I squeezed my eyes shut and remembered our first kiss. The snow all around us, the way he slid my hat back, and kissed my forehead. Everything about it was so perfect. Just like our life together had been.

And now, here I was: without him. I recalled Christmas last year and felt panic rising inside me when I realized how close it was coming. A second Christmas without Andrew would be as excruciating as the first was. I wouldn't have his help with the stockings, the tree, the boxes of ornaments, presents. All of it.

Suddenly, I struggled to remember what Andrew's face looked like and felt myself gasping for air while tears fell out of my eyes like rain. My mind felt disorganized with thoughts and feelings. I refocused my thoughts to my breath and counted inhales and exhales to pull myself back to reality. It took minutes, but I felt myself recover.

 I placed the crane on the grave next to some flowers his parents had placed earlier with the kids. There were a few other flowers from friends and relatives who had come earlier in the day. I was touched by the outpouring of love even though I was tired. I made myself remember sitting in the hospital and ran through the feelings of shock I experienced when I first heard the news and saw his body. I felt sad, yet empowered. I had overcome so much this past year and felt hopeful.

I remembered that I hadn't had a panic attack in or near Andrew's closet in two weeks and felt strong, although the feeling didn't stay with me for more than a moment. I didn't cry audibly again until I brushed some of the flowers to the side so I could read the dates. I made the connection that I was now older than Andrew would ever get to be. 31 was too young to die.

I arrived home from the cemetery and looked at the front door of my house. I was hopeful that Ruth would be standing there as she had been exactly a year ago. No one was home and I felt my heart sink. I was exhausted and lonely. I longed for someone to hold my aching bones. My tired soul and body were spent from the emotions of the day...from the entire year. I had intentionally not reached out to Matt. I felt too guilty even though I know I didn't have any reason to.

I fought back a fresh set of tears as I unlocked the door

and wandered upstairs to my own closet. It was so quiet, so dark, and so lonely at home. If Andrew was home, it wouldn't have felt like any of those things. We would have been laughing, dancing, playing with Miles, rocking baby Lydia. Making paper cranes. We would have been doing normal things that a husband and wife would do during the week. I wouldn't be standing alone in my own closet, staring at my wedding gown. I wouldn't have collapsed on my bed after the hot bath I had taken while I just stared at the wall in front of me, completely numb. I wouldn't be crying. I knew for a fact, a big fact, that there was no possible way I'd be crying alone in my house on a weeknight if Andrew was still alive.

If he was still alive I wouldn't be crying, but if I had been for any reason, Andrew would have pulled me onto his lap, let me bury my face in his chest, and held me until every tear was dry and I was laughing again. He'd let me pour out my heart to him and I'd hold his hand against my lips afterwards, grateful to him for his very presence. But he wasn't here so I didn't get to laugh even once.

I didn't know it, but across the graveyard, standing in the parking lot, two people had been watching me from just yards away earlier as I knelt by the headstone and set the paper crane on top.

"Are you going to tell her or should I?" Ruth asked.

"I'm working on it." Matt replied.

Chapter 15

CASSIE

"You've reached the voicemail of Ruth Hodgekins at Trask, Sepler and Roe Law Firm. Please leave a message and I'll return your call as soon as I can. Thanks and have a great day!"

Again, two weeks after the anniversary of Andrew's death I was greeted by Ruth's voicemail instead of her actual voice. I had called her at least 100 times, sent her text messages, and even called crying to Jennifer about why Ruth wouldn't talk to me. Jennifer knew of no reason but was sympathetic to my plight.

At least things with Matt had been going really well. Once, we met up on a Thursday morning for breakfast in the city before he went to work now that Widow Wednesdays had all but dissolved. He came over two other nights and agreeably watched Disney movies with me, Miles, and Lydia; we held hands in secret under the blanket. We hadn't kissed since that night in the basement. I felt fine about seeing Matt and about my growing feelings for him, but kissing him again, so soon after my graveyard date with Andrew just felt a little wrong. I explained this to Matt and he was more than understanding.

Matt smiled as he pulled me onto my living room couch after I tucked the children into bed one Friday night. He hooked his arm around me, leaned down to my right, and kissed my cheek.

"You're so beautiful." he whispered in my ear with a smile.

"Don't say such wonderful things to me, Mr. Brooks." I said with a sigh.

"It's hard not to. Why shouldn't I?" he asked, a little puzzled, but unable to rip his eyes off of me.

I sighed again, my heart feeling oddly heavy.

"I'm feeling sort of weird." I admitted, turning toward him.

My legs were curled underneath me and I reached for the glass of bourbon Matt had set on the coffee table for me while I ran to get Lovely to give to Lydia in bed from the other room minutes earlier. He always seemed to know exactly what I wanted.

"What do you mean?" he asked with a little concern on his face.

I pressed the side of my body back into his so that he understood I wasn't feeling *that* weird. He felt strong and warm, perfectly holding me up. I leaned my face against his chest. I felt so protected.

"I think just being at the graveyard got me a little sad again…if that makes sense. I still want you to be here, though. I really, really do. Does this make any sense?" I hurriedly explained.

"Of course it does. It was a graveyard, Cassie: there's nothing more sad than that. I completely understand." Matt said, his voice calm and warm.

I loved the sound of his voice over my head, the deep tone and the vibrations of it pulsed against me. I leaned into his neck; he brought his hand up to the side of my head and ran his fingers through my hair slowly.

"I got home that day and felt super sad and lonely. Last year, Ruth was here waiting for me and now she won't even speak to me. I cried a lot..." I explained, trying to brush it off a little bit, not wanting to linger on the topic of death if I could help it.

"I'm so sorry, Cassie. I know it might have been weird to call me on that particular day, but please know that I would have happily talked to you about literally anything you wanted that day." he said.

He said the best things to me. It was so encouraging.

"Matt. You're the most wonderful person. Thank you for saying that. You're right though, I couldn't have called you that day. I would have felt so guilty. It really sucked though. Really, really sucked." I admitted, before sipping my drink once more.

Matt looked down at me intently while he spoke to me and tenderly tucked my hair behind my left ear.

"I never want you to feel like you have to hide or downplay any feelings around me. I can take whatever you have to say. I understand how hard this past year has been for you." he explained quietly.

"Don't you worry about me hiding emotions, Mr. Brooks. I share my range of crazy with everyone I know. You've probably already seen me at rock bottom and sky high…" I explained

with confidence, knowing that what I was saying was the absolute truth.

I didn't hesitate to throw back another large sip of bourbon
at the admission. He hooked his arm back around my shoulders and gave me a squeeze. He kissed the top of my head and
let me sit and sip my drink in blissful silence. I was surrounded
by warmth and glowing light. He had no idea how much it
meant to me that he could be patient, and how encouraging it
was that I didn't have to feel lonely in my thoughts. He listened
to me and understood me, not needing to question the way
I felt. He never told me how to feel or what to think. I threw
back my last sip of bourbon, reached up to his warm face, and
planted a kiss on his cheek. He smiled at me while my heart
melted a little bit.

"You're really cool." I whispered into his ear.

"You are cooler." he replied.

"I can't be considered 'cool' anymore, Matt. I have kids." I
said with a smile.

"I disagree completely. My mom was really cool and she
had a kid. Plus, you're a young mom. A hot mom." he said.

I took in his genuine smile again and beamed back at him.

"You got me, Mr. Brooks." I admitted.

I felt the bourbon sink in a little further and my
bravery rose.

"I'm not lonely when I'm with you, Matt." I said in a quiet
and serious tone.

I watched his smile grow.

"I'm not lonely when I'm with you, Cassie." he replied.

"Were you lonely before?" I asked.

"Only a little. I'm used to living alone." he said.

"I can't remember what it's like to live alone, but I'm not used to some other things." I said.

"Like what?" Matt asked with a genuine curiosity.

I inhaled as I decided what I should and should not cover in my answer.

"I'm not used to cooking for one adult instead of two. Or going to little school events by myself. I'm not used to seeing one car sit in the garage untouched for months. There's so much less laundry to fold now. There's no masculine presence…" I explained.

Matt looked at me, still curious.

"No masculine presence?" he asked.

"No deep voice to settle the kids when they're hyper. No one to open the jars. No one to help me fold the ladder back up when I get on the roof and clean the gutters. No one in bed next to me. No one to replace batteries when they die…the list goes on and on. It's weird." I explained.

Matt looked at me wordlessly for a long pause while he took in my words.

"You've gotten up on the roof by yourself to clean the gutters?" he asked.

"That's what you got out of that?!" I exclaimed.

Matt laughed.

"I'm sorry! I just feel astounded! It seems like a bad idea; your roof is really high, Cassie!" he exclaimed.

"Well, I guess I'm not afraid of heights! Someone had to do it! You see how much rain we get here! I was perfectly fine, as you can see: I'm still here…"

"Cassie. Next time you need a masculine presence that involves height, electricity, or heavy lifting, please don't do it yourself. Let me help you." Matt insisted.

"Noted." I said plainly.

"Do you need me to change any light bulbs or open any pickle jars while I'm here now?" he asked, half joking.

I laughed and shook my head.

"I'll make you a list for the next time you come. It will take you weeks." I said.

He smiled mischievously and raised an eyebrow.

"Can I add my own items to the list?" he asked.

"I can only imagine what you'd add, Mr. Brooks…"

I rolled my eyes and smiled. He leaned in close to my left ear and whispered.

"I don't think you can imagine, Agent Bond…"

Matt looked quite pleased with himself for his little comment as my eyes widened and my face went serious. My heart began to beat faster. I swallowed and I found just enough courage to speak back to him. I leaned into his ear, making sure my lips were barely brushing it as I whispered slowly.

"How do you know I haven't already?"

Matt looked stunned. This time, his eyes widened and he swallowed. He stood up from the couch and walked into the kitchen without looking at me until he had filled up a glass of water and had drained it. From the distance of the kitchen, he shook his head and half-smiled at me. I raised an eyebrow at him, knowing I had won the conversation and felt a ridiculous sense of pride.

On the days we couldn't see each other, we emailed each other. We sent each other plenty of emails throughout the week because phone calls weren't easy with children underfoot.

4:14pm
FROM: agentcasbond@hotmail.com
TO: matt.brooks@tmbf.com
SUBJECT: Rescue me, My Darling?

Dearest Matt,
Please take me anywhere as far away from my
kids as possible. They're driving me crazy and
won't stop asking when you'll be back to see The
Tree again. I need you to rescue me.
    Agent Cassie Bond

6:13pm
FROM: matt.brooks@tmbf.com
TO: agentcasbond@hotmail.com
SUBJECT: That's my favorite new nickname.
What should I call you?

Dear Agent Bond,
I can rescue you anytime! I have a special
assignment for you though. On the third Thursday
of November, you have to appear at my apartment
in Pittsburgh for Thanksgiving. I don't know how
to make turkey and I need your special set of
skills to accomplish this task. Will you accept
this challenge, Agent?
    Love, Agent Matt????

9:15am
FROM: agentcasbond@hotmail.com
TO: matt.brooks@tmbf.com
SUBJECT: I can't think of any suggestions.

Dear Agent Matt,
I'm not calling you that. It doesn't work.
Agent Bond

9:35am
FROM: matt.brooks@tmbf.com
TO: agentcasbond@hotmail.com
SUBJECT: Beautiful.

Dear Agent Bond,
    I'm crying on the inside but I won't let
it show. I always wanted to be a secret agent
and now I never will be. When I see you next I
think I'll need some sort of comfort. If I kiss
you again will you turn me into the officials,
Agent?
    Love, Matt
    P.S. Please say you won't. I can't wait to
see you again.

3:50pm
FROM: agentcasbond@hotmail.com
TO: matt.brooks@tmbf.com

SUBJECT: "Beautiful" only works as a nickname for a horse. Not a mom.

Dear Matt,

I almost typed "Agent Matt" but it's just so, so stupid and I can't bring myself to do it. I can't make you an agent. It's never going to happen. But luckily for you, you don't have to be a secret agent to kiss me again. I will give you special civilian permission. It's the same authorization Miles and Lydia have. Well...not the exact same...Please, please kiss me again! It's probably obvious and completely self explanatory but, clearly, I'm feeling less weird now.

Are you having a good work day? I'm not. It's boring and I think I just want to make candles in my garage like I did when I was in high school. I bet I could cover my mortgage if I pedaled enough jars of "Balsam Fir" and "Christmas Spice" this season....will discuss with you later at dinner. Can't wait.

Agent Bond

5:04pm

FROM: matt.brooks@tmbf.com

TO: agentcasbond@hotmail.com

SUBJECT: Our first fight? I whole-heartedly disagree, Beautiful. I'll always call you this.

```
Dear Agent Bond,
I'm leaving to pick you up in five. Be ready
or I'll set the restaurant on fire. I can't wait
to see you, four days is too long to go without
seeing your face. I don't think I'll be waiting
until after dinner to give you that kiss you're
hoping for. Leaving soon.
    Love, Matt
```

I had some more success with clearing out Andrew's closet. I made myself Whiskey Sours three nights in a row and tackled everything but the stack of sweaters. I saved two of Andrew's nicer suits in case Miles would want them for any reason in his adult life. I held onto Andrew's watch in case Lydia would want it for her future husband. I tucked away a few nostalgic T-shirts and placed his watch next to his wedding ring in my jewelry box. It all went just fine and felt right.

I was so proud of myself when I hauled all the other clothes to the donation center down the road from the library one Saturday morning. It felt like such incredible progress from even just a month ago.

Tangible progress. You go girl. Making yourself and Dr. Amdell prouder than ever.

Matt arrived right on time on Wednesday night to pick me up for dinner. My heart fluttered as I saw him approaching the open front door as I stood leaning against the frame.

"Mr. Brooks. Hello." I said in a forced calm tone, enjoying the view walking toward me.

He held his navy blue peacoat closer to his frame as he walked on the flagstone path feeling the cooler air outside. The temperature had dropped significantly this past week so naturally, Matt was wearing the perfect weight coat. He looked as amazing as I felt. As his eyes met mine, his face lit up.

"Cassie." he said quickly.

His smile was big with sparkling teeth and deep lines. He quickened his pace after giving me a not-so-subtle once over. I had my tan trench coat on with black heels so he must have caught a glimpse of my feet. He scooped me up entirely off of my feet into a big hug and actually swung me around half way. I inhaled his scent and felt butterflies in my stomach. I hadn't expected to feel this exhilarated.

I opened my mouth to greet him but couldn't release any words. He had moved in on my face so quickly, I hadn't even seen him coming. He pressed his lips into mine and as his hands gripped the back of my shoulders, he lowered me in a slight dip. I pressed my lips back against his and opened my mouth slightly. He wasted no time opening his mouth wider and really deepening the kiss. I felt sparks come directly out of my heart, through my trench coat, and explode with the sparks shooting out of his heart against mine. There was no denying the chemistry between us. My body was like a melted candle and I was like warm wax in his hands; he knew it, and he loved it. Matt pressed me back against the doorframe where I was leaning before. We kissed in the empty space of my open front door for minutes before tearing away from each other.

"Do we have to go to dinner?" he asked, nearly begging as he came up for air.

I laughed.

"Yes. I'm starving!" I declared.

His eyes widened as he smiled again.

"OK, OK. Let's go." he said as he took my hand.

I locked my front door with one hand before I let him pull me down the flagstone path to his car in my driveway.

"Take me to dinner, Driver." I said as I buckled my seatbelt.

"Agent Bond. Am I just your chauffeur?" he joked.

"Only if that's all you want to be, Mr. Brooks." I joked back.

He looked at me, right in the eyes, practically into my soul.

"I want to be much, much more than your chauffeur..." he said.

I blinked.

"Is that so?" I asked slowly.

"It is." he said with a serious tone and expression.

A shiver went down my spine at his confidence. I hid my smile at his bold revelation.

We drove to the city and walked around in the chilly air after dinner. I clung to his left arm as we walked. Both of my arms were practically folded into his for warmth.

"Isn't this close to where you live?" I asked.

"It is." he said.

"Point out your building."

"It's right over there." he said as he pointed to a tall building to the left of me.

It overlooked the river and would have made for a gorgeous view of the city lights at this time of night. I didn't mention it though, because I didn't want him to think I was insinuating I wanted to go to it.

"I have to know when I come help you make a turkey."

I joked.

Sort of.

"Oh my gosh, are you really going to come? I wasn't really serious. What are your Thanksgiving plans?" he asked, his eyes wide with nerves.

"I don't really have any. I sort of hate Thanksgiving now because it wasn't super fun last year for obvious reasons. The kids don't even like Thanksgiving food. We didn't even celebrate it last year." I explained.

"So what are you going to do?" he asked.

"What are *you* going to do?" I retorted.

"Me?!"

"You!"

"Me." he said in a resigned tone.

"No pressure by the way. You said you wanted to be a secret agent, well, here's your chance. You can earn agent-status by cooking." I said.

Matt's eyes went huge as he took in my neutral face.

"My chance?!" he exclaimed in fake outrage.

"Yes. Don't worry, I'm sure you won't blow it. It's only my least favorite holiday that holds many, many depressing and soul-crushing memories of death and feelings of panic and anxiety…there is no possible way you can screw it up." I smiled.

"Oh my gosh. I feel so much pressure…Please, Agent Bond. Don't put this on me!" he half-laughed and appeared shocked that I was really expecting this.

"I have full faith in you, Mr. Brooks. There are plenty of tutorials on YouTube of how to cook Thanksgiving dinners for a large group of people." I said matter of factly.

"LARGE group of people!? How many 'people' are in this 'group'?!" he asked.

"Just me, Miles, Lydia, my parents: Janet and Bob, my in-laws: Frank and Beth, Jennifer, her husband, baby...a few other friends, potentially my friend Ruth. You're also allowed to invite some friends." I said, quickly adding everyone up on my hands.

"Are you serious?!" he asked.

Matt looked a little panicked. It was too much fun.

"If Ruth even bothers to call me again that is; let's say she doesn't come. If my math is correct, which it always is, that leaves you with 24 guests, assuming none of your friends make it, then it will be more. Will that many people fit in your apartment or should we set you up with an apron and turkey baster in my kitchen?" I asked.

Matt's laughter was the best sound I'd heard all night.

"Cassie, are you serious?!"

"Why shouldn't I be?!" I asked innocently.

"OK. Here's the deal, Agent Bond," he said as he stopped walking and faced me head on.

"I'll make you a Thanksgiving dinner and I'll make it for as many people as you want me to make it for, BUT, I'm not doing it unless you promise to help me more than just a little bit." he said.

"No deal, My Friend." I said.

Matt looked shocked.

"No deal?!" he exclaimed.

"No way. I believe in you, Mr. Brooks. I know you can do this without my help. I will agree to bringing exactly one side dish as a contribution." I teased.

We both couldn't help but laugh.

"You're something else. You know that?" he smiled and laughed as he pulled me closer.

"Oh, I absolutely know that." I said plainly.

He grabbed my face, his fingers moving into my hair. He wasted no time. He placed his warm lips on mine with boldness. His tongue was desperate for mine. I linked mine with his over and over, running both of my hands through his hair. I felt my chest rise and fall with my own desperation. I gasped as he tipped my head back toward the right and sucked my neck, taking his mouth from under my ear, back down toward my shoulder. I felt goosebumps spread across my entire body. He pulled my loosely buttoned coat off of my shoulder as much as he could, exposing it to the cold night air. He sucked and licked the top of my bare shoulder blade before moving across to my collarbone. He lingered there before going back up to my mouth. We inhaled at the same time and pushed into each other's faces even closer. I grabbed the sides of his face with impatience.

A chilly gust of wind blew across us, but my wet and exposed shoulder was the only part of me that felt the chill. His lips, his hands, and his face were the perfect temperature and I couldn't get enough. I wanted to feel his arms again and ran my hands up and down them, over and over. My entire body felt plenty warm where we stood. Minutes passed before we pulled away from each other, both of us out of breath, but smiling.

I couldn't believe how much more interesting Matt had become to me each next time he kissed me. Every time was more intense than the time before. I dwelled on it for longer than I should have as we turned around. Matt reached for my hand to hold as we began to walk. He brought my hand up to his mouth and kissed it, making it feel significantly warmer than the other hand in the pocket of my trench coat.

"OK. I've thought of the perfect exchange for my hand-made Thanksgiving for over 20 people." Matt declared as we headed in the direction of his car.

It was time to head home.

"What's that?" I asked skeptically, still trying to shake off the exhilaration that still consumed my entire body from our kiss moments before.

"You have to go rock climbing with me once. If you do this, you'll get the best Thanksgiving you've ever experienced." he promised with a sly smile and a twinkle in his eyes.

It felt like he was talking about a lot more than side dishes and the promise of seeing him in front of the stove all of a sudden.

"Mr. Brooks! I'm a married woman!" I said with a gasp.

I batted my eyelashes, but he wasn't falling for my widow act. He held up my left hand and raised an eyebrow along with the corners of his mouth. My fingers were devoid of the rings I'd worn for years and had been for months. I was no married woman anymore and we both had never been more fully aware of it.

"I see no rings." he stated.

"Busted."

"Rock climbing. That's the deal." he said with an eyebrow raised.

"Fine. But I'm not going higher than five feet and you aren't going anywhere below the carabiner belt."

It was my turn to raise an eyebrow at him. Matt blushed at me calling him out and smiled.

"Agent Bond. How could you possibly think my intentions are anything but pure? Also, how did you know what a carabiner was?" he asked.

"Take me home, Driver. You're about to be demoted to chauffeur status forever." I said laughing.

Matt drove me home, holding my left hand in his right hand as I reluctantly set a date in my calendar on my phone to go rock climbing at some freezing cold state park an hour away. I was already dreading it but knowing Matt would be there made the notion somewhat bearable.

Matt pointed out the very tall building his foundation had settled into and caught me up on the latest about his doctor friends and job. It felt natural and as though we'd driven to and from the city catching up on our lives and work for years. I felt light and free, completely devoid of any of the weird feelings I'd felt weeks ago.

After we kissed goodbye, I had to *rip* myself toward the inside of my house and away from Matt's embrace. He looked like he was in a daze as I waved to him and backed away. He put his hand on his heart and pretended to have been shot, his face in fake agony.

"Drive carefully." I reminded him.

"I will." he said, looking suddenly serious.

I couldn't take my eyes off of him as I backed away. He was so gorgeous in his navy peacoat.

"I had so much fun tonight. Matt, I'm so glad you're not boring." I told him from a three foot distance in the doorway.

He looked at me for a moment longer, a serious look still on his face. He almost looked stern, even with his eyes twinkling brightly in the light from the porch lanterns.

"I'm so smitten with you, Cassie. You have to know that. I need you to know that." he said in an exhale, stepping back a half step.

I stood there silently because I had no idea how to respond and my heart began to race. He saved me from having to say anything.

"Sleep well." he said as he turned and walked down the flagstone path.

"Sleep well." I barely whispered to his back as he walked away.

I leaned against my front door and watched him drive down the driveway, feeling the cold air nip at my exposed skin. I touched my shoulder where he had kissed me. I had loved it. A shiver went down my spine as I recalled Matt's intense passion. The way he kissed me, the way he looked at me, the way he said he was smitten with me. I felt my heart beat faster, smiled, and opened the door to walk inside.

Chapter 16

MATT

"You've reached the voicemail of Ruth Hodgekins at Trask, Sepler and Roe Law Firm. Please leave a message and I'll return your call as soon as I can. Thanks and have a great day!"

I heard Ruth's voicemail before I left her a brief message telling her to call me back as soon as she could.

It was late on Wednesday night right after I had returned to my apartment after dropping off Cassie. I still had to tell Cassie what needed to be said, but now, I was so caught up in my feelings for her and in the plans I was making with her, that I couldn't bring myself to say anything at all. The past weeks, reconnecting with her, dating her, were changing my life in almost every single way. I had never experienced feelings like this of any kind and I didn't know how to navigate what should happen next.

I decided I'd have to drive to Ruth's office in the morning. I needed to tell Cassie before her feelings caught up to mine. I could handle another let down, but I'd do anything to avoid putting Cassie through anymore heartbreak. She deserved so much better and I had to be honest. I needed to talk to Ruth as soon as possible.

Chapter 17

MATT

"Jack, I want to be honest with you about something so please listen carefully."

I was standing in Richardson's office on Thursday morning. Before heading to Ruth's office, I knew it was important that I came clean with him.

"What's up, Matt? You look so weird. Where are you going right now?" Richardson asked me with a puzzled expression.

"Listen. Jack. I'm seeing Cassie Caldwell and I think it could really be something. I wanted to tell you now because I'm on my way to Ruth's office downtown and I felt like I needed to let you know before I talked to Ruth. I need to tell Cassie everything that's going on and I can't wait any longer. My feelings for her have become very, very real and I didn't want you to feel blindsided." I confessed.

Jack looked appalled.

"Wait? You're dating her? Cassie? Caldwell?! My old college girlfriend? With the dead husband who..." Jack said, his words trailing off.

He scratched his curly hair and paused.

"This is weird, Matt. I'm not gonna lie. With everything that just happened with her husband and how you--"

"I know. Trust me." I cut him off.

Juan walked in humming to himself, interrupting both of us.

"Oh hey Matt, I didn't realize you'd be in this early. I needed Richardson to sign something really quickl--"

"Did you know about this, Doc?" Jack cut him off sharply.

"Know about what?" Juan looked lost.

"That our golden boy here is seeing that dude's widow, Cassie Caldwell...? Don't you think that's a little insane with everything going on, Juan? Did you know this already?" Jack asked, not breaking eye contact with Juan.

"Listen, I think we should relax. I'm on my way to tell her that--" I said.

"You know I dated her years ago, right?" Jack said to Juan at an attempt for context even though it didn't apply to anything currently going on.

Juan stood in between us looking confused. Anger rose inside me and I forced myself not to let loose.

"Listen! This doesn't have to be a big deal. I just want to be honest with her. I know that honesty comes as a new concept to you, Jack. You've been claiming my solo sail story was yours for ages." I snapped.

Jack looked at me with his mouth hanging wide open and

his eyes confused.

"Sorry. Forget I mentioned it, Jack. I'm a little stressed about having to talk to Cassie and it would be great if you could both be on the same page with me. This is happening." I said apologetically.

"I completely get that, Matt. I just don't want to see you get involved in something that could really blow up in your face. I already know more than I want to..." Jack said.

"I have this under control, Jack. I just explained that to you." I said.

My arms were spread wide open as I tried to get it through Jack's head that I had made my mind up. Juan's head turned to the right and left, over and over, as he watched my exchange with Jack.

"It's all going to work out. I'm tired of lying to her and I don't want to withhold anymore than I already have, Jack. Please just trust me on this one." I said.

I walked out of the room in a hurry before the conversation with Jack could turn anymore sour or he convinced me to change my mind.

"You dated that girl Cassie? Is that why you're mad at Matt?" Juan said to Jack with a look of confusion.

"No. Why would I be mad at him about that? It was ages ago. Juan, I'm literally married with two kids..." Jack said with crossed eyebrows.

"Well, what are you worked up about then?" Juan asked.

"Haven't you been paying attention to what's been going on for the past year?" Jack answered.

"Oh...that! Is it that thing that has to do with that lawyer, Ruth?" Juan asked.

"He's on his way to her office right now. He's going to tell Cassie everything..." Jack said with a serious gaze and walked out of the room.

Chapter 18

CASSIE

"You've reached the voicemail of Ruth Hodgekins at Trask, Sepler and Roe Law Firm. Please leave a message and I'll return your call as soon as I can. Thanks and have a great day!"

I was getting beyond hurt by Ruth's inability to answer my phone calls or even text me a response of any kind as I tried calling her phone again on Thursday morning only to hear her voicemail for what felt like the millionth time. At this point, I would have been fine with a one word answer. I had so much to talk to her about and the feelings of confusion she was leaving me with were breaking my heart.

We hadn't spoken in weeks and I hadn't seen her in over a month. I wanted to resuscitate Widow Wednesday. I wanted to see her, to hug her, to know what was new. I really needed her on the anniversary of Andrew's death; that was a major day for her as well and we didn't even speak to each other on it. I was hurt and confused. Jennifer had at least confirmed that Ruth was still alive by telling me they had exchanged a few texts. She was unable to get any real information out of her though. I was disappointed but I didn't want to put Jennifer in any position that she didn't need to be bothered with. This was obviously a Ruth and Cassie issue that needed to be solved by Ruth and Cassie. Jennifer had more important things to do than to be in the middle of a dispute between myself and Ruth.

I tried for weeks now to grapple with whether or not it was something I had said to her during our last Widow Wednesday. I thought I did a good job not making it all about myself. That morning I was intentional to make it all about Jennifer and her life. *Have I been selfish? Have I hurt her in some way?*

Finally I'd had enough. I was going crazy. I decided that I was going to just drive to Ruth's office instead of working today. I needed to sort this out and I needed to sort this out now.

I had been thinking about what Matt said to me the night before. He had been so real with me about his feelings. Honesty was a character trait I really respected in people and instead of showing him that, I froze up. I decided to send him a quick email before I left for the city.

9:02am
FROM: agentcasbond@hotmail.com
TO: matt.brooks@tmbf.com

SUBJECT: none

Dear Matt,
I am also smitten with you.
Love, Agent Bond

I hit send and pushed in my desk chair. In a rush, I found a pair of cropped black dress pants and my same black heels from last night. I slid on the closest coat next to me after considering the chilly day. My black pea coat was in the front of the closet. I had accidentally dressed as though I was going to a funeral, but I didn't have time to change. I grabbed my keys. I had a few hours until I had to get the kids from preschool, so I quickly headed to Ruth's office.

As I drove into the city, I pushed aside any harbored resentment toward Ruth and instead remembered how magical last night with Matt had felt. I felt proud for being honest with myself. I didn't hold anything back and wasn't in denial about what this was between us. I even considered the possibility of a fun Thanksgiving this year. Maybe there was a crazy chance that Christmas wouldn't suck either. It was at least fun to dream about.

I parked in the garage, collected my ticket at the machine around the corner, and walked toward the elevator. The doors began to close when I shouted for whoever was in it to hold the door and quickened my pace in my heels. *This was a stupid choice in footwear today...*

The doors were almost completely closed when a man's hand appeared and pulled one of them back, opening both doors simultaneously. I was looking down at my heels so I wouldn't slip as I stepped into the elevator. When I looked up, I glanced up at the man who kindly held the door open for me to thank him. It was Matt.

"MR. BROOKS!" I exclaimed with delight and surprise.

With his phone in his hand, Matt looked up at me, surprised and with an unreadable expression of shock.

"Cassie!"

He could hardly speak. He must have been so caught off guard to see me in the city during the day.

"What are you doing here?!" I asked with a huge smile, embracing him with my both arms.

He wrapped his arms around my entire body.

"Umm..." was all he could muster.

He leaned down to kiss my cheek before stepping back to look at me. He was wearing a black suit with a skinny black tie. He strangely didn't have a coat for such a chilly day, but he had still never looked more handsome. To see him in the city so unexpectedly, with his blonde hair, bright blue eyes, and handsome face in this black suit was a sight for sore eyes. I decided to tell him just that.

"You're a sight for sore eyes: so handsome! What are you doing here?!" I asked again, taking his hand in mine.

"Cassie...umm...I'm, I'm meeting someone..." he seemed unsure of his answer.

I felt a little concerned.

"What floor are you going to?" I asked, still wondering why he hadn't grabbed me for a kiss or even another hug.

He couldn't get enough physical contact with me last night so it was odd he wasn't even smiling at me.

"19. You?" he asked without even looking at the panel of buttons.

The 19th floor button had already been pushed.

"19." I slowly replied, feeling my heart racing a little.

He said nothing in response but looked as though he was trying to think of something to say. I dropped my hand out of his and shoved it in my coat pocket. He said nothing and didn't try to take my hand back. I detected a coldness about him I had yet to experience.

"You're acting a little strange, Matt. Is everything OK? I'm going to see my friend Ruth. What are you doing on the 19th floor?" I asked tentatively.

He began to stammer and shift uncomfortably and kept breaking eye contact with me when I heard the elevator ding and felt the doors open. I said nothing, but kept a suspicious eye on him as we both walked out of the elevator falling into step heading the exact same direction. My heart began to pound as we walked.

First, we turned left out of the elevator, then made an immediate right, and walked exactly five doors down a long hallway. This took us to the outside of my best friend Ruth's office. I had this path memorized for years ever since she took this job. I had walked this way countless times: when she won a case and I brought champagne, when I got engaged, when she was made junior partner, when she couldn't get out of the city and I had brought her lunch, when Jennifer and I would surprise her with hot dogs from her favorite place, when she was having a hard week.

I knew the path in this building as well as I knew Ruth. We had years and years of close friendship history behind us but for the first time, as I stood outside of her office, slowly and quietly knocking in case she was on the phone, I felt like I didn't know who the person was on the other side of the door.

Matt was still mute and stood awkwardly to my left, out of sight of Ruth should she just crack open the door. I had let him remain quiet for long enough and needed to know what was going on. It was so tense, standing in between Ruth on the other side of the door, and Matt on the other side of the planet. He was in his own world and I was done trying to work out why in such a quiet and polite fashion.

"What the hell is the matter with you?" I hissed, turning toward Matt.

I glared at him, giving him a five second window to answer me. He remained silent and looked bewildered. My frustration with him rose to a new level.

"Why aren't you saying words? What are you doing here?" I asked, my heart beating quickly inside of my chest with mild rage.

Before he even had a chance to respond to me, Ruth swung the door open all the way, exposing the two of us standing with strange looks on our faces in the hallway.

"Cassie!" she nearly shouted, looking completely stunned.

She blinked unnecessarily for seconds as she processed the sight of us. Her eyes moved back and forth between Matt and I more times than I could count.

"Ruth. What's going on? Why haven't you answered any of my calls?" I said as I got right down to business and ignored Matt behind me.

I walked right into her office without waiting for a signal. Matt and Ruth exchanged a look I couldn't describe. I was done with the secrecy and was desperate for answers.

"What the hell is Matt doing here and why have you dropped off of the face of earth, Ruth? This is the longest time in over 12 years we haven't spoken!" I exclaimed.

I was so angry I couldn't believe I wasn't swearing at her.

"Cassie. Let me explain…" Ruth started to talk.

Instead, Matt finally decided that he remembered how to speak a human language and cut her off.

"No. It has to be me." he said quickly.

I turned to face the general area where the sound of Matt's voice had escaped.

"Oh hello, Sir. Welcome to the party." I snapped at him as I gestured for him to take a seat and make himself comfortable.

We all remained standing.

Ruth gave him a sympathetic look making me want to punch her in the face. I actually didn't know who I wanted to punch in the face more: Matt or Ruth. My frustration and now, rage, rose to a new level.

"One of you better open your mouth and start talking right now or so help me God I'll smack you both in the face with my bare hand. This is ridiculous." I spat out, almost shaking.

I was pulling no punches and I no longer cared how insane I sounded.

"Maybe you should sit down, Cass…" Ruth suggested.

She looked like she was near tears. I immediately shook my head.

"No chance in hell." I declared, still seeing red.

She could cry all she wanted but I would not be made a pathetic fool.

"Cassie. I have to tell you something and it isn't going to be easy to hear." Matt said, having finally stepped up and remembered how to speak with coherent words.

"Please continue. Actually, please *start*." I said, my arms crossed.

I prepared myself to absorb a confession of betrayal that would amount to Ruth and Matt secretly hooking up like the way she did with her old boyfriend Jared in college before he was officially single. Jared had charmed her into dating him before dumping his actual girlfriend, Jasmine Renoylds, and it was embarrassing for everyone involved. I primed myself to be Jasmine Renolylds as I stood with my arms crossed. I didn't know what I would do, but I had no problem using verbal attacks on people who hurt me in the past so this wouldn't be any different. I swallowed and fully readied myself to yell at each of them individually.

"There's no easy way to say this...Cassie. Cassie, I. I'm responsible for Andrew's accident." Matt said.

I don't know which of us looked more taken aback. Matt looked like he was in physical pain, and I felt so confused by what I was hearing that the room actually started spinning.

"What...what did you just say?" I asked without breathing.

"I blame myself for Andrew's accident. It wasn't supposed to happen, Cassie. It could have been completely avoided but the drunk driver who hit him was my dad and it's completely my fault. Cassie, I have been so sick over this...you have no idea." he said.

"I have 'no idea'?..." I asked, slowly exhaling.

I was completely shocked. Not to mention insulted.

"Cassie, my dad really fell apart after my mom died all

those years ago. My foundation ships the medical equipment to the hospitals where it's needed. We needed drivers and he seemed like he was doing well..." Matt continued.

I felt my vision go blurry as my imagination dashed to the end of the explanation. I saw Andrew's mangled body in front of me right there in Ruth's office. Suddenly, I could perfectly remember what he looked like. I saw him lying on the floor as though it was the hospital bed. Blood, shards of glass, bits of plastic, metal, and dirt covered the floor in front of me. Andrew laid before my feet with broken bones and bruised skin. His clothes were destroyed, shredded in places, exposing his ripped flesh. I could perfectly visualize his hands. Still perfect. His ring shone in under the fluorescent lights of Ruth's office. I forcibly ripped myself out of this daydream/nightmare combination as Matt began to speak again.

"He promised me he was done drinking. And he was, Cassie. He really was. I thought he was fine. He came to my apartment before he told me he was shipping to a hospital in Pittsburgh and he seemed sober. He had been doing so well, Cassie. He was completely normal. It was me, Cassie. I'm responsible because I shouldn't have let him drive. He shouldn't have been working..."

Matt had to stop himself. His face was dark and solemn. His blue eyes looked as though they would burst with tears any second.

I imagined his dad drinking an entire bottle of vodka hours before stepping into a truck and slamming into Andrew's car. I imagined Andrew trying to swerve, brake, do anything to avoid an oncoming tractor trailer. I imagined the fear and the pain he felt in that moment. I could almost feel the impact of the truck slamming into me, killing me instead. I felt the color drain from my face and my stomach dropped to my knees. My hands were cold, yet sweating, and my eyes felt as dry as a desert. I swallowed and blinked to make sure that I was still alive.

I perfectly remembered what Andrew's distorted face looked like while he lay on the hospital bed. It looked nothing like the face that I promised myself to never forget when he went in to kiss me under the snowy tree that day in college. That face was so perfect, so kind, so genuine. It was the face I looked directly into on my wedding day and promised to share my life with. It was the face I saw every single night when I closed my eyes. It was the face that I saw in Miles and Lydia every single morning when they greeted me. Now it was broken, coated in blood. It was burned, split apart. Dead. That was the version of Andrew's face I kept seeing when Matt continued speaking.

"Cassie, you have to understand, you have to understand that I never considered anything like this would happen. I completely trusted what he said. I was so sure he was fine. I never dreamed anything like this would happen--"

"You never imagined!" I cut him off, starting to gasp for air.

I blinked and swallowed again, standing up straight before I continued.

"You never imagined something like this would happen! What the hell did you think would happen?! You set an alcoholic driver behind the wheel! How did you think it would end, Matt?! You actually thought everything would be fine?" I shouted.

Tears stung in my eyes as I yelled.

"Cassie, I seriously just wasn't thinking and I haven't forgiven myself since. You have to know how this has torn me up inside…" he pleaded.

"'Torn you up inside'?" I harshly repeated his words back to him.

I had never been so insulted by someone's ignorant comment in my life.

"You think it's torn you up? Do you have any idea how your lack of forethought has affected so many people's lives? Matt. I've had to rebuild my entire life. Do you know what it was like telling my kids that their Daddy died? Do you know what that was like for me? Did you imagine it when you saw them for the first time? What if his mom was here right now? Do you know what it's like to bury your son? Do you know how much pressure is on me as a single parent? Matt, do you know anything?"

My voice had cracked in the middle of my thoughts. I was crying so hard and had shouted so loudly, that I could barely speak by the end of my last question. I couldn't look at him anymore. I slowly spoke my last thought to Matt before I turned away and reached for the box of tissues on Ruth's desk.

"You killed him all over again for me here, Matt…" I said as I gestured to the floor where I'd been reliving so many horrible images this entire time.

Ruth stepped near me. I still didn't know why we were in her office for this conversation. I had completely forgotten where I was. All I could picture was Andrew's coffin being lowered into his grave while my mother-in-law collapsed at my side. I remembered holding her up on one side of her while my father-in-law was on her other side. I couldn't hear anything except for the moans of agony they let loose in the hospital when they saw their bloody, broken son beneath them. I pictured my kids in their small funeral clothes, watching their father's coffin be covered with brown dirt. I remembered shivering in the windy graveyard, trying to hold it together for everyone else around me.

I brushed Ruth's hand off of my shoulder as I snapped back to reality once more and wanted answers from her now. Matt had said enough and now it was her turn to explain something.

"What the hell do you have to do with any of this? Are you sleeping with him?" I asked in a demanding tone.

I was so upset in so many ways, I couldn't even say Matt's name out loud.

"No." she answered quietly.

Ruth was crying so she was unable to say anymore than that. I handed her the box of tissues as though I was the one who worked in this office.

"Cassie." Matt rushed to explain.

"If you already hate me now, it's only going to get worse. Right after the police called me and told me about the accident, and who was killed in it, I called my lawyer. You know Jack. Jack Richardson. He's still my friend and he works for my foundation. When I told him where the accident was and mentioned Andrew's name, he immediately recognized it as your married name. He looked online and saw that it was definitely your Andrew. Jack told me how you had kids, how little they were... Cassie, you have to know that I didn't even believe it at first... I wanted to die when I saw whose husband my dad had run into... I couldn't believe it was you. I couldn't believe something like this would happen to someone like you, someone I knew..."

Matt was overcome with emotion as the confession continued. I began to sense his genuine grief over the entire situation and fought off the urge to both punch him and hug him. I swallowed back both ideas.

"Jack suggested that I get some local legal counsel to handle everything because no one wanted bad press for the foundation and it wasn't his specialized area of law. It was a truck with my foundation's name on it, my dad, drunk and dead behind the wheel, and your husband was killed. It was a potential legal mess. Jack gave me Ruth's number; he remembered meeting her and that she was pre-law when you were roommates with her in college. She specializes in getting people out of bad press; she made sure no ones names were released on my end. I'm so sorry, Cassie. I shouldn't have kept this from you and I shouldn't have covered it up at all. I'm so, so sorry. I don't know what else to say." Matt said with desperation.

It made so much sense now. I'd never be able to know the name of the person who had hit Andrew. There were a ton of hoops to jump through and red tape that I wasn't able to navigate. Ultimately, I decided it didn't matter who the driver was and gave up trying. I knew it wouldn't bring Andrew back or offer me any peace, and I didn't see the merit in pursuing a settlement or anything. I was financially fine and wanted to move on with my life rather than being tied up in court, instead of spending time with my grieving children.

Then, out of the clear blue sky, I received a check for a disgusting amount of money from a law firm I had never even heard of. I had asked Ruth what it was and she explained to me that it was a sort of 'non-settlement-settlement'. She encouraged me to keep the money and that obviously, whoever caused the accident had felt compelled to give me something as an act of benevolence for not pursuing a lawsuit. I was confused about it at the time, but now it all made sense.

The money had come from Matt, desperate to alleviate his guilt and grateful that his foundation's name would not become the focus of bad press and death. My feelings blended together as the information swirled in my brain. I hated that so much had been hidden from me from my best friend for a year and that I was somehow Matt's charity case without even knowing it.

"Ruth...you knew? You've been his lawyer this whole time covering this up?" I asked.

I looked away from Matt and directly into Ruth's eyes.

"Yes, Cassie. I knew the day after Andrew died that Matt knew you. I couldn't say anything. There's laws...I just...I didn't want you to get hurt. I didn't want you to ever find out..." Ruth stammered.

"Ruth advised me not to send you that letter. She told me it would be a huge mistake to get in any kind of contact with you. But Cassie...I had to see you in person. I had to tell you. You deserved to know and I meant to tell you the first time I saw you. I just couldn't do it. I'm so, so sorry." Matt said.

He wiped tears away from both of his eyes and looked like a complete mess.

"Is that why you didn't put a return address on it?" I breathed out.

It was all I could think to ask.

"Yes. I figured I would just put it out there and that maybe it would work out and maybe it wouldn't. I just knew that I had to try." Matt said quietly.

He inhaled, trying to regain himself.

"When you emailed me again, after all those years of bearing my soul to you, I couldn't just ignore it. I had to see you." he said.

Matt looked visibly ill as he spoke.

"Why didn't you tell me? Why didn't you tell me all this before now, Matt?" I pleaded.

"I tried." he barely whispered.

"You didn't try hard enough." I said plainly.

I turned to look at Ruth.

"And you. You broke my heart, Ruth."

I turned to walk out of the office I no longer recognized. I didn't know this office anymore and I didn't know the people in it either. They were strangers to me. Ruth finally spoke up as I stepped one foot out of her office into the hallway.

"Cassie. I wanted to tell you so many times. I wanted to keep you away from Matt and I tried to discourage you. I'm so sorry. Once he told me how hard he had fallen for you, I told him I wouldn't keep his secret anymore. It's why I didn't pick up your calls and answer your texts. I got to a place where I couldn't keep client confidentiality so I stopped all communication with you. Cassie, I didn't want to, but it had to be done. Cassie, please don't walk away. I wanted to talk to you, I wanted to see you...I even went to Andrew's grave. I saw you there and I wanted to run to you..." she explained with conviction but was still crying.

I stopped breathing as she spoke.

"Andrew's grave? You saw me there? Why wouldn't you have told me, Ruth?! Do you know how hard it was to come home, remembered you being there the year before? I was a complete mess, Ruth. I needed you!" I shouted through tears.

"That's also my fault, Cassie. I told her not to go over to you. I knew you wanted to be alone." Matt chimed in out of nowhere.

I looked directly into Matt's eyes.

"What are you talking about? Why the hell would you have been there?" I spewed.

I could not recall being this angry with anyone else in my entire life. Kneeling in front of Andrew's grave was such a personal thing for me. It was so difficult, so horribly challenging.

"You aren't the only person who lost someone on that exact day last year..." Ruth whispered.

I couldn't even look at either of them anymore. *This is pathetic. Three grown adults crying in a law office...*

I walked away without looking back at either of them. I had nothing more to say. I heard Ruth burst into a fresh batch of tears in her office as I walked down the dim hallway. Matt's footsteps got louder right behind me as he got closer. I didn't look back and instead pretended the person I'd started to fall for wasn't there at all. I didn't ask to be a part of a mess like this. I had never felt more determined to pick up Miles and Lydia and hold them in my entire life. I wanted to tell them that they were the only people in this world I'd ever need.

"Cassie, wait!" he said as he came up next to me.

He wisely didn't try to grab my hand.

"For what?" I asked flatly without looking at him.

"Cassie, let me drive you home." he said.

"Do not follow me."

I made it to the elevator and smacked the button to open the doors.

"Cassie. I wanted to tell you so many times. I am so sorry.

Please don't leave like this." he begged.

The doors opened and I stepped on with him close behind me.

"Why are you here?" I asked him still avoiding eye contact, although it was hard not to look at him.

"I don't think you should drive home like this. You're upset." he said.

"You don't get to tell me how I feel, Matt! I've had to figure out my feelings by myself for a year until you showed up and ripped my heart back open! You have just undone so much of the progress I have worked so hard for! You have no idea how hard it is to have someone close to you taken away in the blink of an eye when you aren't expecting it and then you have to figure out how to rebuild your entire life from the ground up!"

I was back to shouting with rage at the top of my lungs as we walked off the elevator and into the parking garage. I looked Matt in the face, not realizing the words that had just come out of my mouth. Matt knew this pain. He knew how it felt twice over. I was so heartless. I thought of his mother's handkerchief and felt a little more sick to my stomach. Then I thought of what it would have been like for him to receive the news of his father. I had completely forgotten that I wasn't the only one who had lost a loved one around this time last year. Thanksgiving probably sucked for him as well. Not to mention Christmas.

I had been selfish, but not with Ruth, with Matt. I had been shortsighted and insensitive; I had never even asked him how his father had died and now I was connecting that the anniversary of Andrew also would have been a difficult day for Matt. I imagined him acres away from me in the graveyard, kneeling in front of his father's headstone with confused feelings of guilt and grief.

Ashamed of myself, I turned my face away from Matt's solemn eyes and continued walking to my car. This time, I figured I'd be walking away alone for sure. Matt stayed near as I unlocked my car from a few feet away. He opened the driver door for me without saying anything. I took the car door from him and turned to face him one more time.

"I'm sorry. I realize that that day would have been horrible for you as well. I shouldn't have said those things just now..." I said quietly.

I spoke slowly so that he would know that I did regret what I had said, but my anger was still a very real presence. Matt said nothing as a response and looked at me with a neutral expression.

I got in and sat in the driver seat and slammed the door closed. I noted him step several feet back in the corner of my eye. He stood with his head down and his hands in the pockets of his black suit. All of a sudden, his slim fit suit looked huge on him. He looked thin and pale, his features sharp and tired. I pulled away without taking my eyes off of him in the rear view mirror. Matt hadn't been boring to me before, but after the past hour, he proved to be the least boring person I'd ever met. I almost felt relief amid my anger and sadness.

Chapter 19

MATT

I stood motionless as I watched Cassie drive away in the parking garage. Probably for the last time. Her words were cutting and definitely stung but I deserved every sentence. My phone buzzed in my pocket. I slowly pulled it out while I held my gaze on the exit of the parking garage. I looked down and saw two missed calls from Ruth and a notification of an email from agentcasbond@hotmail. It had been sent just two hours ago. *She probably sent this right before she left.*

```
9:02am
FROM: agentcasbond@hotmail.com
TO: matt.brooks@tmbf.com
SUBJECT: none
```

```
Dear Matt,
I am also smitten with you.
Love, Agent Bond
```

I closed my eyes with exhaustion and longing after I read her email. I had blown this entire thing up. She was starting to fall for me and now I'd never know what we could have had. I felt numb emotionally and physically. I fought off visualizations of Cassie explaining to Miles and Lydia that their father was never coming home again.

I called Juan to let him know I'd be back to the office soon.

"Hey, Juan. It's done." I said.

"What happened?" he asked.

"I told her everything but I'm pretty sure I lost her for good. You were right about it being hard. I was just hoping it would also be great." I confessed, attempting to sound light-hearted.

"I'll be here when you get back." Juan said.

I found my car in the garage, sat in the driver seat, and rested my head against the steering wheel for just a moment. I must have fallen asleep because it said three on the clock in my car. I sighed and adjusted my seatbelt to drive away. I went to set my phone in the cup holder and realized Cassie's email was still pulled up.

Chapter 20

CASSIE

It was a weirdly warm Saturday when I got out of my car in the middle of the woods. I was sure this was the place I had saved in my calendar so I grabbed my water bottle, zipped up my light windbreaker and walked down the dirt path. The trees were bare but the sun was bright and reflected off of the nearby creek. I walked for at least five entire minutes until I found the large clearing of woods below me dotted with people in colorful athletic clothes, coolers, bags of gear, and rope strewn on the ground in front of the face of an absolutely gigantic rock. *Let's do this. Let's see what all the fun is about. Maybe there's a lesson here...* I rolled my eyes when I saw a few people strapping into harnesses, attaching their water bottles to loops on their side, and taking pictures of themselves halfway up the rock.

"Hi." I said as I approached someone who looked to be essentially a college sophomore, holding helmets in one hand

and a cigarette in another.

He was wearing what looked like a hooded sweatshirt made out of burlap and short, bright purple biker shorts. He sported a mustache not dissimilar to the monopoly man's. I deduced that this was the person in charge of this climbing area of the rock.

"Oh hey there! Are you here to climb?!" he asked with the voice that could only be described as a voice of an excited yet also stoned skateboarder.

"Umm...yes. What do I need to know? I have never done this before." I told him.

I didn't actually want to do this, but I had this day free of children and I was starting to become more and more curious about something I knew I'd hate. It had been a strange few days since my awkward and explosive interaction with Ruth and Matt. I decided that even though I'd hate rock climbing, and even though Matt wouldn't be joining me, that the great outdoors would serve my mental state well. Plus, Dr. Amdell had told me to try new things and I wanted to prove to myself that I was right about what I thought about rock climbing for all these years and that it was completely stupid. This would give me firsthand proof of how pointless it actually was.

"OK that's awesome! I'm Ralph! I'll get you set up! Let's get you strapped in! Have you ever done this before?!"

Ralph started asking questions about my skill level of outdoor sports and explaining safety protocol. I was immediately bored and only half-listened.

I set my water bottle down next to a small rock and stepped into what was essentially a diaper made out of colorful ropes while Ralph rambled on. So far I was right on this being dumb.

How hard can this be? You strap yourself to this rope and move the pulley. So easy a caveman can do it.

"...and that's all you need to know! You got this, Girl! Have fun and make sure to like us on Instagram!"

Ralph had evidently just wrapped up an entire spiel about this climbing organization after giving any and all instructions I should know about. I probably should have paid closer attention but I wasn't planning on going very high and how hard could it be to go five feet up the side of rock?

I went all the way to the further side of the face of the rock away from everyone else. They looked experienced and annoying so I wanted to keep my distance. Plus, I didn't want to end up in the background of some college students' selfie, so I looked straight in front of me focusing on the little metal hooks and the ropes next to me. I hooked my fingers onto a piece of the dark gray, cool, hard rock and found my footing easily.

I ascended a few feet after getting a literal hang of where to grip and step. I pulled the rope, hooked the carabiner and shimmied myself upward with success while using lots of muscles I didn't know existed. I could tell I'd be sore later. It was physically difficult but didn't feel like anything special. *Definitely nothing life changing about this so far.* I continued up the rock and started to think about Matt, Ruth, Andrew, even Jack...*he would have loved this.*

Matt would have loved this. He would just lose his mind if he knew that I was rock climbing all on my own after everything. All the insults I hurled about how dumb this was over the years would be shoved right back in my face right now if anyone knew I was here doing this. Life is weird...

"Umm, what are you doing?" I heard Ralph shout up toward me as I climbed.

"What does it look like I'm doing, Ralph? I'm rock climbing." I replied down to him without blinking.

College students were so stupid.

"Umm, yeah. I see that, except you are way, way high right now..."

He sounded concerned from down below.

"Trust me Ralph, no one is higher than you my friend..." I shouted as I rolled my eyes.

"No, seriously, you're like 25 feet off the ground..." he said.

I looked down and saw that what Ralph was calling 25 feet, actually looked like 100 feet from where I was. It felt nothing like the time I had cleaned out the gutters.

I glanced in the direction of the other rock climbers and saw that they were all lower than me on the rock with expressions on their faces that ranged from being impressed to concerned.

"What the hell, Ralph? How did I get up here and how am I supposed to go back down? Why did you let me get this high?!" I shouted down to him.

This was definitely Ralph's fault.

"I can't come get you...like...you'll have to come down by yourself or whatever...I thought you said you'd never done this..." he replied.

"Of course I've never done this, Ralph! Do I look like the kind of person who ascends rocks in their spare time?!.." I yelled down.

"So what are you gonna do?..."

Ralph sounded so unqualified, it was ridiculous

"What am I 'gonna do'?! You're the professional, Ralph! Why

don't you TELL ME what to do?!"

"Just do the same thing you did when you came up, except go back down..." he shouted with a tone of such little confidence, it almost sounded like a question.

"I only meant to go like five feet, Ralph! I don't think it can be that simple." I replied.

"It really is that simple...you gotta just do it."

"A quote for the ages, Ralph. This is so stupid. Do you have any other suggestions for going back down?" I asked.

I was losing patience with Ralph and his non-answers. I was hoping he'd say that if I just went up another four feet, then there would be a spa or something at the top and you could walk down a dirt path to the base after a shoulder rub and a few sips of a Nalgene filled with Gatorade.

"Just do what you did when you went up, except this time you're gonna come back down. It's basically the same thing, you just have to be braver..."

Ralph had no idea how wise his words were.

"Just be braver?" I shouted down in earnest.

"Yeah...you gotta be brave. You gotta just do it."

"K." I inhaled.

I slowly tightened the rope and stepped downward. I hooked the carabiner into the next small metal hook. I exhaled. I'd gone down about three feet. Only 22 more to go...

Ralph was right. You did have to be braver to get back down. It required so much more effort than going up. It was physically quite difficult but the real challenge was mental.

While I slowly descended, Ralph said incoherent words to me the entire time. He rambled on about technique and how they did this every Saturday morning.

Once I touched down on solid ground again, Ralph walked over to me and helped me unhook. I heard some of the other climbers shouting and cheering in my direction.

"That was amazing!"

"You sure you aren't a professional?!"

"Sick!"

"That was insane! You rocked it!"

A few people were even clapping.

I ignored the individual shouts of encouragement and instead gave the entire group a little bow as a collective thanks for their kindness.

"You did it! Up top!" Ralph said as he held up his hand and I reluctantly gave him a high-five.

He deserved it.

"Ralph, thanks so much for your help, but I will not be sending my children to whatever summer kids program you mentioned earlier." I said.

I handed him my harness, an extra 20 dollar bill out of my pocket, and grabbed my water bottle. *This was an overall success...what did we learn?*

My arms, legs, and stomach were already sore as I walked up the dirt path. The parking lot looked like a beacon of light by the time I made it to my car. I took my phone out of my cup holder and saw no new notifications. My heart longed to see a missed call or text from Matt. I sighed and drove home in the sunshine knowing I'd learned nothing and would definitely need a painkiller for all my unknown muscles.

Chapter 21

MATT

I hadn't spoken to Cassie in days. I really wanted to, but I knew she needed space. I wasn't exactly sure what to do next other than what I had always done when I needed someone to talk to and had no one available. I got out of bed, pulled on jeans, but didn't waste my time with a shirt. I poured myself a cup of coffee in my now perfectly organized kitchen and carried the hot mug over to the office. Sitting in my desk chair, I sat up straight to type properly as I composed an email to my favorite email address.

7:23am

FROM: matt.brooks@tmbf.com

TO: agentcasbond@hotmail.com

SUBJECT: Please read this.

Dearest Cassie,

You'll probably never read this, or if I'm lucky, you'll read it in ten years.

I'm sorry. I know there's nothing I can say to change the past. I'm sorry I didn't tell you that I had a crush on you years ago. I'm sorry I didn't just call you after my mom died. I'm sorry I emailed you all those times when I could have just seen you in person. I'm sorry I was such a coward then and I'm sorry that I've been such a coward now. I shouldn't have covered everything up. It was wrong and I'm so, so sorry.

Please don't blame Ruth. I told her so many times that I'd tell you. I just couldn't bring myself to do it. When I saw you standing outside of that smoky diner in the rain, you looked so beautiful and so sure of yourself. Everything I loved about you in high school, even from a distance in college, came flooding back to me. You had slipped between my fingers before and I finally had a chance. I never meant to withhold anything from you; I just never had much of a family and you were letting me into yours so warmly. I had no idea how good it felt. Miles and Lydia are so lucky to have you as their mother.

Andrew was so, so lucky to have you. He didn't deserve to die in such a senseless way. I will never forgive myself for not stopping my dad; I knew he had a problem, but I did nothing and if I could explain to you how much that has eaten me alive for every single day of this past year, I would. It would be pointless though Cassie, because your loss has also been great and you were so blindsided. I just want you to know that my dad wasn't a bad person, he just never got over my mom's death. He loved her so much and was never going to be the same again. The only comfort I have is knowing he isn't suffering anymore and the fact that he will never know what happened because he also died, helps me in a strange way.

Andrew was obviously an incredible person if you chose him to be your husband. He had the best of everything and I'd be lying if I didn't tell you how jealous I am that he got to have years with you.

Cassie, I know you might not ever forgive me, but if you think there is ever a chance, even a small one, please, please take it. Please take a chance on forgiving me. I am so hopelessly in love with you. You have become everything I ever imagined you would and I'm so impressed with you. I love you, Cassie. Please, please forgive me. You don't have to love me back, you don't even have to speak to me ever again if you don't want to. I would just be happy to be near you, to know that you didn't hate me forever. I would be happy just holding your hand.

Love, Matt

There was almost no chance she would read it and even if she did, there was definitely no chance Cassie would forgive me anytime soon. I scratched my head in frustration and thought about the few times I had the pleasure of kissing her. She had trusted me to be the first person to date, to kiss, after her husband had died. It was such a high honor. I tried to secure the feeling in my mind so that I would never forget what she tasted like in my mouth or what she felt like in my arms.

Chapter 22

CASSIE

Widow Wednesday was here, except that it was actually on a Wednesday morning this time. Jennifer wasted no time hiring a babysitter for Lucy and demanded that Ruth and I get ourselves to The Back Country Diner. I had never seen Jennifer so fired up and motivated to leave her house. She told me she was totally on the ball about coming this week.

I really missed Ruth and was appreciative to Jennifer for making this particular Widow Wednesday happen. I parked in front of the diner and remembered all of our fun days in college. A waterfall of memories crashed down. Ruth was everything to me. She was waiting for me on the front path of my house when I drove home from the hospital after Andrew's accident. I remember her calm face as she opened her arms to me and held me while I sobbed for hours on the couch. She always stayed up late in college talking to me about boys, classes, clothes, anything at all. She knew how to deal with my complicated personality and gave it back to me when I needed it. I didn't know many other women like Ruth who were both confident but also wore their heart on their sleeve. Ruth didn't have much success with romance, but she was the most loyal person I'd ever had the privilege of being best friends with. One day, the right man would come along and be so, so lucky to have her. On my wedding day, she was there helping me zip up my big white dress and then years later zipped up my funeral dress. I wept at the thought of both days as I sat in my car.

Dabbing my eyes with a tissue, I noticed a car pull up next to me. It was Ruth. I got out of my car and walked over to her without hesitation.

"Ruth. I've missed you so much. I'm sorry. I'm so sorry you were caught in the middle of everything--" I said.

"Cassie. No. I'm the one who's in the wrong here. I shouldn't have kept this from you. I should have told you that Matt approached me. I should have told you about Jack Richardson approaching me for legal advice the minute it happened. I didn't know what to do. Matt's company is doing such amazing things so I didn't want it to get bad press, and I could see that he was such a great guy...I just knew how hard this would be for you and I hated lying to you." she explained.

"Ruth, can we please, please, never go this long without speaking again? I hated it so much and I didn't have you to call after all the fun stuff with Matt. I'll probably never have that fun again now..." I realized aloud.

"What makes you say that? You've always known exactly what you want. If you want to be with Matt, you can make that happen Cassie." she said.

She looked confused as she stared at me.

"What do you mean?" I asked.

"Cassie. You're obviously falling for him. Why don't you take a chance and just talk to him?" she asked.

She made it sound so easy.

"I don't know Ruth...it's a lot..."

The parking lot was chilly as we still stood next to Ruth's car. She was making really good points though. I did always know exactly what I wanted.

"Do you want this with him?" she asked me plainly.

Ruth wasted no time forcing me to answer myself as she posed the question. Such a lawyer.

"Yes. I want this. I want this with him." I noticed myself answering without hesitation.

"Good. Make it happen, Cassie. I know you'll find a way." she said.

"You're the best cheerleader of my life. Do you know that?" I asked with a smile.

Ruth nodded at me with a smile.

It felt like we were completely back to normal. Ruth and I both looked around the parking lot hugging our coats tightly around us.

"Where's Jennifer?" I asked.

"Jennifer's supposed to come?" Ruth asked.

"Oh my gosh. She's such a liar. She told me she was definitely coming this week." I said.

I rolled my eyes, realizing she wasn't going to come and that she was probably laughing to herself while she snuggled her baby in her warm living room an hour away.

"So are we still eating?" Ruth asked.

"Not here. I know another place. Have you ever tried The Other Diner?" I asked with a smile.

Ruth looked unsure.

"Isn't that the place that caught on fire?" she asked.

"Yes, but if the crazy lady on the sidewalk, (no, not me, the other one), was willing to wait 45 minutes in the rain and sit in the smoke to eat there, it must be incredible. It's time for something new." I said, linking my arm in hers.

"I'm down!" Ruth said with a smile.

We left together and had the best sandwiches we had ever eaten at The Other Diner. Even though Jennifer wasn't there, it was one of my favorite Widow Wednesdays of all time.

Chapter 23

CASSIE

Thanksgiving came and went with Miles, Lydia and I eating pizza, singing songs about turkeys, and falling asleep on the couch. Life felt as though it had mostly gone back to normal except for the fact that I thought about Matt every single day. I convinced myself that I was perfectly fine to not eat turkey and mashed potatoes. I didn't need a huge gathering to feel normal this year. I could keep it low key. I could be boring for one year.

A week after Thanksgiving, I slid out of bed and crept downstairs to the computer. I hadn't checked anything but my work email in weeks but because it was a Thursday, I thought about Matt the minute I'd awoken. I had waited long enough to talk to him. I couldn't lie to myself and deny how much I missed him, and after my conversation with Ruth, I knew that I wanted to see him. I just didn't know how we could continue on the path we started before everything blew up in Ruth's office. I said hurtful things to him that I wished I could take back and he withheld so much information from me for so long. My heart ached thinking about everything that had happened. It took a lot of mental energy for me to get my mind around Andrew's death being Matt's father's fault.

I didn't even know who I was mad at anymore. Matt took the blame, but he wasn't the one behind the wheel; plus, it felt wrong to be angry at someone who I'd never even known. I imagined an older, just as attractive version of Matt driving at top speed. My thoughts became gruesome and didn't offer me any peace. I really missed Matt. I really missed Andrew. Things in my head felt complicated even though everything else in my life was feeling normal again. As I gave everything more thought from a public relations perspective, I completely understood why half of what happened was handled the way it was.

I hesitantly logged into my old Hotmail account for the first time since the day I saw Matt in Ruth's office. I had an urge to log in every single day since I saw him there, but just couldn't bring myself to do it. I almost emailed him to tell him that I went rock climbing without him. It would have been more worth it to tell him in person, just to see his reaction. I smiled at the thought.

There was one unread email. My palms began to sweat and my heart began to beat faster when I saw that it was from Matt. I felt excited and nervous. After I read the entire email four times in a row, I circled my finger over the keyboard for minutes until I finally clicked the reply button.

```
6:34am
FROM: agentcasbond@hotmail.com
TO: matt.brooks@tmbf.com
SUBJECT: I read it.
```

```
Dear Matt,
    I just read this. Aren't you glad I didn't
wait for years? Can I see you again so that we
can talk?
    Cassie
```

I held my breath and waited for over 30 minutes in the hopes of a reply. None came so I went upstairs to take a shower. I decided that I might as well get something accomplished if I wasn't going to have the chance to talk to Matt in person. I stepped out of the shower, pulled on some jeans and a white T-shirt, and rushed back downstairs to my computer without bothering to put on any socks. I folded my legs to keep my feet contained and warm as I logged back into my email. Matt had just replied.

```
8:04am
FROM: matt.brooks@tmbf.com
TO: agentcasbond@hotmail.com
SUBJECT: I am so happy you did.
```

```
Dear Cassie,
    Yes. I am so glad you didn't wait for years
```

this time. I fully expected you to and I'm happily surprised. When and where?
    Love, Matt

    8:10am
    FROM: agentcasbond@hotmail.com
    TO: matt.brooks@tmbf.com
    SUBJECT: Me too.

Dear Matt,
    I don't want to wait another week until I'm
free in the evening. Tonight or tomorrow night
are both fine but Miles and Lydia will be here.
Maybe wait to come until after they're in bed.
Can you come over at 8:30?
    Cassie

    8:17am
    FROM: matt.brooks@tmbf.com
    TO: agentcasbond@hotmail.com
    SUBJECT: none

I'll be there tonight at 8:30.

My hands were shaking and my heart was pounding; Matt
would be here again tonight. I looked to the right and the left
to assess how messy the house was. I had let the tidiness of the

house go a bit now that Matt hadn't been a regular visitor.

There was so much to do, so many things to clean up. I didn't have much time before I had to pick up Miles and Lydia and would find my day occupied by their presence so I quickly touched up the kitchen table, threw the dishes in the dishwasher, put laundry away, and fluffed up the couch cushions.

Later, I picked up the children from school and anxiously watched the numbers on the clock, pacing the house. Finally, when I tucked them into bed, I hid my nerves from them like a champion. I had had so much practice. I went to the front entrance after I came downstairs to turn on the front lights. It didn't look like it was almost 8:30 outside; something about the lighting outside didn't look quite right.

I stepped away from the front door to see if I had left my headlights on or something when my eyes fell onto the ground. It was covered in snow. Every single speck of grass, driveway, tree branch, and shrub was thick with fluffy white snow. There were at least five inches of snow that must have accumulated while I was frantically still cleaning my house and going over the alphabet with Lydia in anticipation for Matt's arrival.

How could I not have noticed it had been snowing? I was perplexed by how quickly it must have fallen. I checked my watch and paced in the kitchen until the clock said 8:30. There was still no sign of Matt. My heartbeat quickened inside my chest as the minutes continued to pass by. I peered out the sidelight of the front door for any sign of headlights. I ran upstairs to check on my kids who were both sound asleep. I shivered and grabbed a cardigan from my bedroom. *I shouldn't be this worried. I shouldn't be this nervous. Everything's fine.*

I was starting to panic inside. Thoughts of Matt blowing me off and not coming at all consumed me for minutes until they shifted to thoughts of Matt's car crumpled on the side of the road. The roads to my house would have been complete slush. So slippery, so dangerous. He used to live in New York City so what if he didn't drive much in snow? He probably walked everywhere. What if someone else lost control and hit him on the road? I had so much to say to him. What if I wasn't given the chance? What if he ended up in a hospital bed and I never found out? Panic rose and my breathing went into a weird pattern. I was inconsistently getting air and was loudly gasping. I needed fresh air immediately.

I noticed the time on the stove before I stepped outside through my back door. It was 9:05. I walked six steps into the snow barefoot, found my snow-covered patio table, held on with my left hand, and dropped my head. My left hand and both of my feet were shocked with cold. Flakes floated from the sky in a rapid flurry echoing my breathing. *If I could just get some air...*

The next thing I heard was the sound of the door opening behind me.

"No shoes in the snow?" someone said behind me.

I gasped in relief, my chest pounding, as I turned around to see Matt standing behind me.

"First you work out with jeans on in your closet and now you're standing in a blizzard without shoes or a coat..." he said calmly as he took another step toward me.

I still couldn't get a full breath of air, but the sight of Matt standing safely near me brought tears to my eyes and warmth to my heart. His entire body glowed with the light of the house behind him. I couldn't make out his face very well in the dark, but the relief I felt of knowing he was standing near me was electric. My gut reaction was to run into his arms. He was here. He was standing so high above me, so tall, so handsome, so warm, and so alive. It was more than I could bear. He saw my attempt to come closer to hug him and beat me to it. I saw his face change from a joking smile to a serious stare as my eyes adjusted to the dark and light combination.

He quickly picked me up. I wrapped my legs around his waist and he pulled me close into his chest with his strong arms. He held me up with ease; I set my head against his shoulder and felt his heart beating rapidly against mine. I instantly felt warm all over. I missed this. I longed to feel his body close to mine. He held me up with his chin nestled into my neck for a moment before setting me down. I stood on the cold patio, feeling wet snow beneath my feet again without letting go of him. I looked up at him under the light for a moment. His blonde hair was collecting snowflakes and his nose looked cold. I felt his jacket under my arms. He was wearing the perfect winter coat; the snowflakes bounced and rolled right off of his arms and back. It looked warm without being too thick. It perfectly complimented his jeans.

"I really, really like this coat." I whispered.

"Can we go inside now?" he asked in a gentle reply.

"Yes."

We broke apart before he reached over and opened the back door before standing back to let me in. I stepped inside and noticed how covered in snow the arms of the cardigan I was wearing became. I couldn't tell which sweater it was at first because I had grabbed it in such a rush. It was Andrew's. Andrew's olive green cardigan I couldn't part with, the sweater that had caused my last panic attack in front of Matt. The brown wooden buttons were damp with melted snowflakes.

"Are you OK?" Matt asked me as he saw me study the sweater.

His voice indicated that he recognized it as well and his eyes looked worried.

"Umm...yeah. I. I am..." I answered.

"Are you sure?" he asked.

He still looked concerned. He probably assumed I was panicking in the snow because of the sweater.

"This isn't like last time, Matt. This wasn't about the sweater. I got so worried...I panicked..I..I thought you..."

I couldn't finish my thought because Matt had me in another embrace.

"Cassie. It's OK. I'm here. The roads were terrible so I had to drive really slowly. I'm so sorry I scared you. I'm so sorry I'm late." he said quietly.

"Stop apologizing." I whispered into him.

It was the only thing I could think to say.

"No, seriously Cassie, I have so many to make..." he started to say before I made a move.

I stepped away from him, slipped Andrew's damp sweater down my bare arms, and set it over one of the kitchen chairs. I stepped back in front of Matt and unzipped his perfectly dry coat for him. Matt obediently took off his coat, hanging it on the back of one of the other chairs. I took his hands and gently pulled him to the living room. He seemed to be reading my mind as he grabbed a blanket from one of the arm chairs. We walked over to the couch, I sat down with my freezing cold feet underneath me again. Matt covered me with the blanket and sat next to me, facing me.

I had control of my breath again and was already starting to warm up under the blanket. The lump in my throat had melted away as I warmed up. It gave me the energy to finally speak a coherent sentence to him. I cleared my throat before I spoke.

"Mr. Brooks. Never apologize to me again." I said slowly and quietly as I leaned forward toward him.

It was all I needed to say. My words must have held so much more for him because his face told me that he completely understood what I meant as it relaxed and his eyes became brighter. I had forgiven him, I was sorry, I missed him, I needed him in my life, I was smitten with him. I could see in his eyes that he understood it all. I didn't need to re-live everything from our past in this moment. He grounded me, he calmed me, and he excited me all at the same time. I wasn't bored with him, even if we were quiet together.

We sat in silence for another moment as Matt moved closer to me. Pressing his forehead against mine, we were still and close. He inhaled before he spoke.

"I love you so much, Cassie." he whispered.

I felt the lump in my throat return. I couldn't articulate any words so instead, I touched either side of his face and kissed him for just a moment, softly and slowly. I ran my fingers through his hair all the way to the back of his head, and breathed him in. He lifted his hands to either side of my face as well and kissed me back, sweetly and lovingly, before he reached up and kissed my forehead.

I woke up on the couch at 5:30 the next morning with Matt's arms surrounding my waist and his cheek on my hip bone. He only had a third of the blanket over him. He was still half-perched on the edge of the couch, with his long legs sprawled partly on the couch and partly on the floor.

I blinked my eyes open and squinted at the dull white light coming in through the window. Matt detected I was awake and opened his eyes quickly. He smiled at me as we caught each other's eyes.

"Let's go outside." I whispered in his ear.

He stood up from the couch wearily and held his hands out to help me up. I took them both and hung on to one of them to lead him to the back door. He slipped his coat on while I grabbed some tall rubber boots and my coat from around the corner in the mudroom. Without speaking, he took my hand again to help me slip my bare feet into them. When he saw that my coat was zipped up, he quietly opened the back door and we snuck outside.

The most gorgeous scene of a thick blanket of snow greeted us as the sun slowly peaked through the trees. The sight of it was incredible and lifted my spirits to a new high. I was so happy. The sky was pink, red, blue, and purple. Matt held my hand while we took in the wonder of the first snow of the season. I brushed my hand against the snow-covered shrubs. It was so perfect. With my free hand, I balled up the fluffy snow as well as I could and threw it at Matt. It mostly fell apart mid-air, but hit him lightly, square in the back. He looked surprised and delighted. His eyes were bright blue and his smile sparkled in the dim light of the rising sun.

"Trying to start a snowball fight this early, Cassie?" he

asked with a smile.

"I told you it would stop raining just in time for the snow to come. I'm going to eat some, do you want any?" I asked him, no longer having to whisper.

Matt nodded.

"Yes, I absolutely want to eat this snow." he said.

"Here, have some of mine." I said as I handed him the remains of my crumbled snowball.

He took the chunk of snow and slipped it into his mouth with an adorably delightful expression. I grabbed more snow for myself to eat from another shrub. I adored the cool sensation and the taste. It reminded me of childhood and I suddenly became so excited for Miles and Lydia when they woke up and saw eight inches of snow in their yard. They would have so much fun. Matt smiled as he reached for more snow from another shrub within reach.

"It's so good. Tastes like winter. My favorite flavor." he said.

"Let's go see The Lightning Tree. Do you think the snow even stuck to it or did it melt right off?" I wondered out loud.

We continued down toward the tree all the way across the yard, hand in hand. The tree came into view with tons of snow on it. I was disappointed that it didn't remain a black stripe amid a white backdrop the way I imagined it would. I turned to express my disappointment to Matt. He looked serious. I wondered if maybe he was disappointed with the sight of the tree looking just like all the others as well. We were right next to it, examining it closely. I noticed him looking at me, not at the tree at all, and looked up at his face. He stared at me, gently pushed me against the trunk, and took my face into both of his warm hands.

Don't forget this moment. Don't forget the way he's looking at you.

As he leaned in, I opened my mouth and felt his cold tongue inside my cold mouth instantly. He tasted like winter. His hands moved up into my hair as his passion grew. His entire body was pressing me further against the tree. I felt his hips, his legs, and his stomach pressing against mine even through our winter coats. My hair was getting covered in the snow that had fallen down the tree trunk.

Matt's face strongly pressed against mine as he moved his mouth from my mouth to my chin, from my chin to my neck. He reached toward my neck and unzipped my coat with shaking hands to just beyond my heart. His mouth, now as warm as he'd made mine, had moved down to my now exposed collar bones. He took his mouth aross my collarbones, grazing the rise of the bone with his teeth more than once, before moving up the side of my neck for minutes. I heard him gasp for air as I ran my fingers through his hair. His hands moved to my shoulders; I could tell he was forcing them to stay there.

"Beautiful Cassie. I'm so smitten." I heard him whisper in between breaths.

"I am too." I whispered back.

We slowly pulled away from each other as more sunlight illuminated the snow around us and the sky became more light blue and less orange. We knew the day had to start and that this moment had to end. We walked toward the house in silence, Matt quietly opened the back door to let me inside. He lingered in the doorway for a moment, not coming inside. I had to get ready for my kids to wake up and he had to head to work. We read each other's minds and knew that this random overnight date at my house was just about over.

"I wish you didn't have to leave." I said quietly.

"Can I see you later?" he whispered with a smile.

His eyes were sparkling from the reflection of the snow.

"I'll email you." I whispered with a smile.

"Goodbye, Beautiful." he exhaled.

Matt slipped me another quick kiss on the cheek and carefully walked through the snow around the side of the house to his car in the driveway. I laid back on the almost still warm couch where Matt and I had fallen asleep. I slipped into a daydream of Christmas not being completely awful this year as I pulled the blanket back over myself and wished that Matt was with me underneath it. I imagined that he would drive to my house in the morning and drink hot chocolate with Miles and Lydia while I made waffles. He would help build Miles' new toy race car track and pretend to be excited about Lydia's new Barbies as he opened them with his knife. We would try to create a signature Christmas drink with whatever we found in the fridge. Maybe even cook a proper Christmas dinner for my parents. I fell back asleep on the couch with Christmas carols playing in my head.

Chapter 24

MATT

My drive home was slow and careful in the snow. The sun was bright, but the roads were an absolute mess. I didn't even care that I had to drive 25 miles per hour all the way back into the city. I was tired but so filled with life and happiness that I felt like I could have stayed awake for another week straight if it meant I was actually with Cassie. I walked through the door of my apartment and pulled my snowy boots and winter coat off. I tossed the boots in the general direction of where all my shoes were stored on a shelf and quickly hung up my coat. The apartment didn't feel like home somehow, but I didn't care. I started my shower so that I could get ready for work and make it to the office on time. I pulled my shirt off and walked over to check my email while the water heated up. I smiled and felt my heart flip over when I saw that there was one new email from Cassie that had been sent just 35 minutes before.

6:40am
FROM: agentcasbond@hotmail.com
TO: matt.brooks@tmbf.com
SUBJECT: Thanksgiving, My Darling?

Dearest Matt,
    Will you come over later? I'm buying a turkey
and I need help making it. I didn't celebrate
Thanksgiving this year and I have so much to be
thankful for.
    P.S. I went rock climbing.
    P.P.S. It was stupid, just as I thought it
would be.
    Love, Cassie

I hit the button to reply.

7:15am
FROM: matt.brooks@tmbf.com
TO: agentcasbond@hotmail.com
SUBJECT: Yes.

Dearest Cassie,
    Happy belated Thanksgiving. Do you always
scold strangers from mid-air or do you only do
it in diner parking lots? I know you went rock
climbing. I was there among all of the "experienced climbers" who's skill levels you complete-

ly put to shame within minutes of arrival. There was nothing stupid about how quickly you scaled up to 25 feet. It took everything in me not to come rescue you, but I knew I needed to keep my space so I stayed about ten feet below you on the other side of the rock like an ameteur.

See you tonight.

Love, Matt

Five minutes passed when I heard one more email pop up.

7:25am

FROM: agentcasbond@hotmail.com

TO: matt.brooks@tmbf.com

SUBJECT: I forgot to mention earlier.

I love you.

My heart burst.

The End

Epilogue

CASSIE

Matt was heading to my house for Thanksgiving from the city. I instructed him to "completely empty the city of all it's ice", just an hour ago because there was none to be found near my house. Widow Wednesday was cancelled for this Thursday so that we could all prepare the massive amount of food in my kitchen that we had planned for Thanksgiving dinner tonight. It smelled so much better than last year's pizza. Ruth shuffled around the stove stirring pots of gravy, while Jennifer sliced vegetables looking very pregnant and barefoot at the kitchen island. Andrew's parents were here entertaining Miles and Lydia. They had decided to paint cardboard turkeys this year for each person's placemat. There were at least 25 other friends and family members coming over in less than an hour.

Matt stepped inside the front door with more bags of ice than I could count in his strong arms. His bright smile and the beard he'd started growing weeks earlier glowed on his face.

"The city is now 'completely empty of ice.'" he declared, setting the bags of ice down on the counter.

Juan and his family were still coming through the door behind him.

"Put those on the floor! They're dripping!" Jennifer said, noticing the wet spots on the counter.

"Oh don't worry, I got it!" Matt said, whipping his mother's handkerchief out of his pocket.

I stuck my hand out, grabbed his wrist, and stopped him in the nick of time.

"Oh my gosh! Don't wipe up the counter with something so special!" I said.

"It's super durable though!" he insisted.

He wasn't wrong. It had been strong enough to handle all the random tears I'd shed over the past year. They were almost always happy tears.

"Don't you dare!" I exclaimed.

I expertly slipped the hanky out of his hand before he could clutch it tighter. I grabbed his other hand and pulled him up the stairs. I opened the door of Andrew's closet, turned the light on, and pulled Matt inside.

Andrew's closet was completely empty now except for the old shoebox of paper cranes I had stored in the back corner. I bent down, carried the box toward us, pulled the lid off, and dropped the handkerchief inside with the rest of the cranes. Matt's eyes sparkled with tears as I stood up in front of him. He slowly took the box out of my hands and set it on the shelf next to us. Obviously touched by my gesture, he took my hands in his and faced me.

"I've kept that handkerchief in my pocket every single time I've seen you since the first time we met again last year and I handed it to you. You? You want to keep it?" he asked quietly.

"Yes." I said, staring into his blue eyes. "I want to keep it forever."

I looked into his eyes as he gazed into mine. We stood in the closet, quietly taking each other in for minutes. Matt pulled me closer to him and held me in an embrace of gratitude. Moments later, we walked out of the closet, I hit the light switch off, and pulled the door shut before walking out of the room behind Matt.

He stood at the top of the stairs with his hands outstretched to me. I reached for both of them but his right hand was closed in a fist. I looked at him with a puzzled expression. He looked serious and solemn.

"What's that matter?" I asked him.

He cleared his throat and stepped closer to me. He opened his right hand up and stood before me wordlessly. I looked down and saw a black velvet ring box. I felt myself shake with nerves of joy.

"What is this?" I asked in a whisper.

Matt gave me a half-smile and extended his hand out even closer to me.

"The right moment." he said.

I watched him bend down on one knee and open the box to reveal a huge diamond ring as I gasped.

"Cassie, will you marry me?" he asked simply.

I nodded and suddenly wished that Matt's mother's handkerchief wasn't all the way in the closet as tears fell out of my eyes.

"Yes." I whispered.

I stepped into Matt's warm, strong arms and kissed the top of his head. He slid the ring on my finger as I caught my breath.

"Cassie, I love you so much." he whispered.

"I love you more." I replied.

He pulled his face away from me and beamed as he looked into my eyes. I gazed at the stunning ring before placing both of my hands on either side of his face; he looked so incredibly handsome to me. He always did. I couldn't believe I would get to spend the rest of my life with someone so perfect.

"This is the best Widow Wednesday of my life...Agent Brooks." I said hesitantly.

Matt looked at me with widened eyes of pure joy and a genuine thrill.

"I'm pretty sure I've waited for over fifteen years to have a Thursday like this. It's the best Widow Wednesday of my life too."

Author's Notes

Writing Paper Cranes was a complete shot in the dark. I had never written a book, but after reading about 30 books in quarantine during the Spring of 2020, I became not only impressed by authors who could write narratives so creatively and comprehensively, but also inspired by the concept of penning a book. My husband challenged me to try it and before I knew it, I had my laptop in my hands and the first three chapters written in a matter of days. I had no idea what it would entail and surprised myself with the level of enjoyment I found in the personal and creative challenges that writing a novel presented.

I had reached a point in my life where I knew of more than one person who's husband had passed away at a very young age while they had young children. Having a husband and young children myself, I was intrigued by the notion that they would have to heal, help their children heal, and rebuild their entire lives. Inspired by this process, and watching some of these individuals fall in love again after tragedy, I thought up Cassie and her entire situation as I tried to imagine myself in the same predicament. Not all widows should be portrayed as withering wallflowers who allow their situation to define them and cripple their entire future. Many are outgoing girls with gumption and a take-charge demeanor, refusing to settle or be pitied.

While there aren't many moments in the book that involve paper cranes, and they may only seem as a bit more than a mention, they amount to bigger symbolism of hope, love, and healing during a time of challenge: the very meaning behind paper cranes.

As Cassie is embarking on her own course of healing during a challenge, Matt also is. I loved the concept that Andrew taught Cassie and their children how to make paper cranes and symbolically set Cassie up for her healing process. The bravery that would be required of both Cassie and Matt after suffering such monumental losses in their lives was also something that fascinated me and was wholly inspired by the young widows I observed in the past several years, some from afar and some from a closer distance. They are an inspiration of strength, surrender, and trust.

Acknowledgements

This book wouldn't be possible without the support and constant mockery from my husband, Tyler. Also thank you to my children for their patience as I attempted to write a book while raising them. Caris: you have been instrumental in more ways than I can count. To my mom and my twin sister: thank you for being the best beta readers who I know will be brutally honest. To my other wonderful beta readers: Hannah, Caitlin and Bailey, (did you actually read this yet?), Autumn, Mindy, Shonda, Olivia, and Samantha.

Thank you to my awesome father for his helpful editing notes; a more grammatically correct man has never been born.

Thank you to Sara for making me pretty and to Kaitlin Powell for the amazing headshots!

Also a HUGE thank you to Jessica: you have brought this to life for me beyond what I dreamt was possible and your creative talent is downright inspirational.

About the Author

Julie James is a first-time author with a love for fun romantic reads that include happily-ever-afters. In her real life, Julie owns a floral design business for weddings and events in Western Pennsylvania. She spends her time raising her two young children with her amazing husband who is very much alive and well. Paper Cranes is her first novel, but not her last.

Connect with Julie at

 @juliejameswrites

 www.juliejameswrites.com

Made in the USA
Las Vegas, NV
03 November 2021